J FIC TAYLOR

Taylor, Chloe

Cute as a button

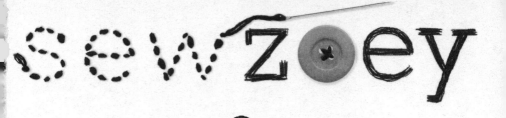

sew zoey

CUTE
as a
BUTTON

written by
Chloe Taylor

illustrated by
Nancy Zhang

Simon Spotlight

New York   London   Toronto   Sydney   New Delhi

This book is a work of fiction. Any references to historical events, real people, or real places are used fictitiously. Other names, characters, places, and events are products of the author's imagination, and any resemblance to actual events or places or persons, living or dead, is entirely coincidental.

SIMON SPOTLIGHT
An imprint of Simon & Schuster Children's Publishing Division
1230 Avenue of the Americas, New York, New York 10020
Copyright © 2014 by Simon & Schuster, Inc.
All rights reserved, including the right of reproduction in whole or in part in any form.
SIMON SPOTLIGHT and colophon are registered trademarks of Simon & Schuster, Inc.
Text by Sarah Darer Littman
Designed by Laura Roode
For information about special discounts for bulk purchases, please contact Simon & Schuster Special Sales at 1-866-506-1949 or business@simonandschuster.com.
Manufactured in the United States of America 1213 FFG
First Edition 10 9 8 7 6 5 4 3 2 1
ISBN 978-1-4814-0248-4 (pbk)
ISBN 978-1-4814-0249-1 (hc)
ISBN 978-1-4814-0250-7 (eBook)
Library of Congress Catalog Card Number 2013943453

--------- CHAPTER 1 ---------

It's Nifty to Be Thrifty

Designing and making clothes is definitely my favorite thing to do, but there's one big catch—buying fabric starts to add up. It's not just the fabric—it's all the trimming, buttons, zippers, sequins—you name it! The only reason I've been able to make so many outfits lately is because of the money I won in the Avalon Fabrics' Break-Out Designer contest—and because both Jan at A Stitch in Time and my aunt Lulu are so great about giving me scrap material. But I'm going from riches to rags, even though I've been doing my best to shop on a budget. My allowance only goes so far, and I'm too young to babysit, so Dad said I can do odd jobs around the house to earn money, but there are only so many of those. Lately, he's been paying me to dust the houseplants and sew buttons on his shirts! What's an aspiring fashion designer bursting with ideas to do? I've been digging around at the thrift store again, trying to find clothes I can take apart for the fabric. But I loved this dress too much to take it apart. Instead I got creative and "Zoeyfied" it. I made some tweaks here and there and added a belt that used to be my mom's. Cool, huh?

"Are you *sure* you don't mind?" Lulu Price asked for the third time as she stood by the door to leave.

"Mind? We love having Draper here," Zoey

Webber, Lulu's niece, said, her arms wrapped around her doggie cousin's neck.

Aunt Lulu's fourteen-year-old mutt thumped his tail against the kitchen floor in agreement.

"See? Draper loves being here too," Zoey said.

"I know he does," Aunt Lulu said, smiling. "This is his absolute favorite hotel. And mine, because I know you and Marcus will give him lots of love while I'm away at the interior design conference."

"Oh, you can count on that," Zoey's brother, Marcus, said. "Draper will get plenty of love—and treats."

"Not too many treats," Aunt Lulu warned. "He's already overweight."

"He is not," Zoey said, covering the dog's floppy ears with her hands so he wouldn't hear. Then she uncovered his ears and scratched the silky hair under his chin. "You are the handsomest dog ever."

Draper licked Zoey's face, as if to agree that he was, indeed, the handsomest dog ever.

"I'll see you in about a week," Aunt Lulu said, blowing kisses as she walked out the door.

Draper trotted over to the entryway and let out a soft whine.

"Aw, he misses Aunt Lulu already," Marcus said. "Give him a treat."

Draper's ears pricked up at the word "treat." Zoey wanted to follow Aunt Lulu's advice for at least a few minutes after she left, but Draper seemed so very sad standing by the door. Just one treat wouldn't hurt.

"Come on, Draper, treat!" she said in a high-pitched voice, walking over to the tin of treats their aunt had left with Draper's food and other supplies.

Draper moseyed over to Zoey expectantly.

"Sit," Zoey said.

Draper stood, staring up at Zoey with his big brown eyes.

"Come on, Draper, sit!" she said again, waving the treat above his nose.

With a deep sigh and an *If I really must* look, Draper sank onto his rear haunches.

"Good boy, good sit," Zoey crooned, giving him his treat.

"I wonder if Draper ever thinks, 'Why do they

make me do this just to get a treat?'" Marcus said.

"I think he just cares about getting the treat!"

"You underestimate him," Marcus said.

"No, I don't. I just think he has his priorities straight. If I could get ice cream whenever someone said 'sit,' I would totally sit down on command! But now it's time to sit and *sew*, right, Draper?" Zoey said.

Sure enough, Draper lumbered up the stairs behind Zoey and followed her into her room. After a brief, unsuccessful search for hidden treats, he settled himself under the cute vintage sewing machine table Zoey's dad had bought her, so she could work in her bedroom. He'd painted the wrought iron pink to match her bedroom. Zoey loved it. Mr. Webber loved having some space on the dining room table for a change.

The week before, Zoey had seen a dress that she absolutely adored in her favorite fashion magazine, *Très Chic*. She wanted it so badly—until she saw the price, which was more than she could ever imagine spending on a dress. But it was *so cute*! That's when she had the idea to make it herself.

With Draper's nose resting on her foot, Zoey sketched out ideas for how to copy the dress. She went online to see if she could figure out what fabric the manufacturer used. For the price they were charging for the dress, she figured it had to have gold thread, but it didn't. And that was a good thing, because unlike King Midas, everything Zoey touched *didn't* turn to gold.

It was comforting to have Draper with her while she worked. He seemed to sense when she was getting frustrated, and he'd give her foot a gentle lick, as if to say, *Don't worry, Zoey. You'll figure it out.*

Zoey put down her pencil and ducked her head under the table to look at Draper. He lifted his nose and wagged his tail, thumping a steady beat against the carpet.

"You're such a good boy, Draper," Zoey said. And then she had a fabulous idea.

"You know what?" she told him. "I'm going to design *you* an outfit!"

She pushed aside the pattern sketches that were causing her so much frustration and pulled her sketchbook toward her, turning to a fresh page.

Soon after, she'd drawn the cutest outfit for Draper and looked online to see what shapes worked best for dog outfits. Now she just had to make it!

Zoey sifted through her box of fabric remnants till she found a piece she liked, and got to work. The biggest problem she had was the fitting. Draper was *not* the most cooperative model. When she needed him to stand, he wanted to lie down and nap. When she wanted him to sit, he wanted to stand. After almost two hours of being measured and man-handled, he was ready to go on strike. He sat his butt on the floor and refused to budge.

"Draper, if you do what I say, I'll give you a treat *and* take you for walkies when we're done," Zoey told him.

Of course as soon as Draper heard the word "walkies," he started whining and heading for the door. Walkies were what Marcus had called walks with Draper when he was a toddler, and the name stuck.

Zoey raced to the door and shut it.

"Not yet! In five minutes! I'm almost done," she promised him.

Draper slumped down by the door, his head on his paws, sulking.

Zoey worked as quickly as she could to finish Draper's outfit. As soon as she was done, she wrangled it onto her reluctant model.

"Draper, you're getting *two* treats and an extra-long walk. It looks absolutely *adogable* on you!" she told him. Opening the door, she headed downstairs to the kitchen and the treat jar, with Draper close at her heels.

Mr. Webber was making himself a cup of coffee when Zoey and Draper bounded into the kitchen.

"Well, look at Draper! When did Lulu start dressing him in designer duds?"

"She didn't," Zoey said. "I made it for him. Just now."

"Really?" her father asked. "That's impressive, Zo. I thought Lulu bought it at the pet store."

Zoey opened the treat tin. Draper barked, and his whole body seemed to wag with excitement, not just his tail.

"Here you go," she said, giving him a treat. "That's for being my model."

Zoey clipped on Draper's leash to his collar.

"I'm going to take Draper for a walk because he was so patient while I made his outfit," Zoey said. "He might need to do his business—and he *definitely* needs to show off his new outfit."

Mr. Webber smiled. "Why do I have a feeling this walk is more about the fashion than the 'business'?" he asked, his eyes twinkling.

"Come on, Draper," Zoey said. "Let's go show off your new duds."

Once they got outside, Draper seemed proud to show off his outfit. He had to sniff every mailbox post and wall they passed, so it was a very, very slow pace.

Zoey texted her friend Kate Mackey, who lived down the street, to see if she wanted to join them.

Yes! ☺ **Be right there!** Kate texted back.

Zoey and Draper walked down to the Mackeys' house and waited outside for Kate.

While they were waiting, Mrs. Lynch came by with her golden Labradoodle, Rusty, who was wearing a dog-size Eastern State University baseball cap and stopped to exchange sniffs with Draper.

"I love your dog's outfit," she said. "Where did you get it?"

"Thanks!" Zoey said. "Actually, I made it."

"Really?" Mrs. Lynch said. "You're very talented. It's so much cuter than the outfits at the pet store."

Just then Kate came out to join Zoey and Draper on their walk.

"Ooh, I love Draper's outfit!" she said.

"I was just saying the same thing," Mrs. Lynch said. "I'd love to get one just like it for Rusty. Do you make them to order?"

"Um . . . no. I never really thought about it," Zoey said. "I just made it today!"

"You should, Zo!" Kate said. "I bet other people would buy outfits for their dogs."

"If you go into business, Rusty and I will be your first customers," Mrs. Lynch said, and then she and her dog continued down the street.

"Draper's so cute." Kate sighed. "Sometimes I wish we had a dog, but Mom says I'd have to be totally responsible for everything, if we got a pet. It seems like a lot of work."

"It is," Zoey admitted. "That's why I love having Draper come to stay with us when Aunt Lulu travels. I get all the fun of having a dog but only a little bit of the work."

"What about doing an outfit for Rusty?" Kate asked. "You could make extra money."

"It's funny you should say that," Zoey said, "because I've been trying to think about my fabric fund. I've almost used up all my reward money from the Avalon contest."

Draper started pulling on the leash, anxious to say hello to an approaching Shih Tzu. It was the most animated he had been all day.

"Hold on, Draper!" Zoey said.

The Shih Tzu's owner smiled at Zoey and Kate. "Looks like puppy love," she said.

"I don't think anyone would call Draper a puppy, but there sure is a love connection!" added Zoey.

"I think Princess likes his outfit," said the Shih Tzu's owner. "She has very good taste. Where did you get it? The Pampered Pooch?"

"Actually, I didn't buy it," Zoey said. "I made it."

"But she's *thinking* about going into business," Kate piped in.

"Wonderful! Well, I'm Mrs. Silverberg. Take my phone number. I'd love to buy one for my little precious," said Princess's mom, giving her card to Zoey.

"I will, promise," Zoey said as she dragged Draper forward.

"See, you already have two customers!" Kate said.

By the time Zoey and Kate had walked Draper to the park and back, Zoey had ten potential customers. After she dropped Kate at her house, Zoey strolled home with a tired, panting Draper.

"You know, Draper, I think you might have inspired me to solve my money problems!" she told him as she took off his leash and got him a treat out of the tin.

Draper took the treat and flopped down on the kitchen floor, exhausted. Apparently, being Zoey's inspiration was very tiring business!

CHAPTER 2

Totally A*dog*able! (Note to Sew Zoey Readers: This Is *Not* a Typo!)

I always love when Aunt Lulu leaves her dog, Draper, with us when she travels, but this time it's not just 'cause he's cute and cuddly and keeps me company when I'm sewing, doing homework, and watching TV. It turns out Draper is my *muse*! I made him this totally adorable (a*dog*able!) outfit. I might even make a matching leash to go with it, but it will have to be industrial strength. Draper might be old, but he's stubborn, and every once in a while he pulls on his leash like he's a young pup!

Anyhoo, when we walked around the neighborhood with Draper decked out in his new outfit, people kept asking me where we bought it. When I said I'd made it, a few people asked if I'd consider making one for their dogs, so Kate said I should start a designer dogwear business.

I think I'm going to see if I can figure it out. I've never really thought of myself as an entrepreneur or anything, but as Dad often says, "Necessity is the mother of invention." And I guess Draper is the dog . . . of inspiration!

Zoey was distracted at the dinner table that evening, wondering how to start her dogwear business. The problem was, she needed money for fabric to make the dog outfits, but she needed to sell the outfits to buy fabric. Also, was it going to take up too much time to run a business? She was already pretty busy between school and sewing and her Sew Zoey blog.

"I saw these really amazing light-up drumsticks on Myfundmaker," she half heard Marcus telling her father.

Zoey started to pay attention, wondering what he was talking about.

"They change color depending on how hard you beat on the drum," her brother continued. "The technology is pretty cool. They've almost raised enough for their project."

"Wait, what is this Myfundmaker thing?" Zoey asked.

"It's a website where creative people put up projects they want to fund through crowdsourcing," Marcus explained. "If you like the project, you can pledge toward it and get different rewards depending on how much you give. Like on the drumstick one, I gave twenty dollars and will get drumsticks and a really cool bumper sticker if the campaign reaches its goal."

"But you aren't allowed to put that sticker on my car," Dad warned. "Because it will ruin the paint."

"I know, I know," Marcus said. "I'll put it on my notebook."

"So if I wanted to start a dogwear business, I could put up a page and ask for money?" Zoey asked.

"What dogwear business?" Dad asked.

"The one I was just going to ask you about," Zoey said. "Draper gave me the idea."

Hearing his name, Draper, who had been lying on the floor next to Mr. Webber, sat up and pricked up his ears, thinking he might be getting some interesting scraps from the table.

Mr. Webber stroked Draper's head.

"Tell me about it, Zo. I'm all ears," he said. "Like Draper here."

Zoey laughed, because Draper's head was cocked to one side, and it really did look like he was listening intently.

"Well . . . so when Kate and I took Draper for a walk, all these people asked me where I bought his outfit. When I said I'd made it, one lady asked if I got it at the Pampered Pooch! So I was thinking . . ."

"About starting a business selling dogs' clothes?" Mr. Webber asked.

"Yes. But the problem is, I'd need to buy the fabric to make the outfits before I can sell them," Zoey said. "So it sounds like I need a Myfundmaker campaign to raise money for material."

"Maybe," her dad said. "But there are a lot of factors to consider when you start a business."

"Like?" Zoey asked.

"First of all, do you know how much it costs you to make an outfit?" he asked. "You need to figure out how much the fabric costs and all the bits and pieces you always end up buying when we go to A Stitch in Time—"

"Notions," Zoey interrupted. "That's what the bits and pieces are called."

"Okay, well, you need to know how much all that costs *and* you also have to factor in your time," he said. "It's going to take you a while to sew each one, right?"

"I forgot about that part," Zoey said.

"You also don't want to forget to build in profit," Mr. Webber said. "I can try to help you, but the best person to speak to is Aunt Lulu."

"Good idea!" Zoey said. "That's the whole reason I want to start the business. The money I won in the Avalon Fabrics' Break-Out Designer contest is almost gone. And what's the fun of designing all these great clothes if I can't make the most of them?"

"I see. Well, let's clear up the dinner dishes and have a look at this crowdsourcing site," said her father. "We can do some market research."

Marcus and Zoey helped their father clear the table and load the dishwasher. Then Mr. Webber got his laptop.

"Okay, let's see . . . What should I search for? Dogs' clothes?" he asked.

"Might as well try that," Marcus said.

Twenty-five projects came up. Zoey's heart sank. She was going to have a lot of competition for her outfits.

"Click to enlarge that one, Dad," Marcus said. "Ewok Dog."

Mr. Webber clicked on the link. The picture was of a little Yorkie wearing a suede outfit with a little hood and powder puff ears.

"That's sooooo cute!" Zoey squealed.

"That is sooooo weird," Mr. Webber said.

"That is kind of hilarious," Marcus said. "What about Yo-Dog!"

The next project was for a Yoda Halloween costume for dogs.

"Poop or poop not, there is no try," Marcus quipped.

"Okay, moving on. Who knew there were so many *Star Wars* outfits for dogs?" said Mr. Webber, clicking on the next picture, which showed a very angry-looking bulldog dressed as a cupcake.

"If *dog* looks could kill . . . ," Marcus said.

"I think he wanted to be a fireman for Halloween, not a cupcake." Zoey giggled.

"Definitely beneath his dignity," Mr. Webber said, moving to the next picture.

There were cat costumes and dog costumes and fashionable pet carriers for teacup dogs, which were the kinds of dogs that celebrities always seemed to carry around in their handbags. But all the pet clothes were more like costumes, not fashionable clothing like Draper's outfit.

"I really could do a page for my designer dogs' clothes," Zoey said. "It's different from what's on here already."

Mr. Webber nodded.

"It does seem like you've discovered an unfulfilled niche," he said. "I'll help you set up the campaign and manage it, but before you put up anything, you have to work out your costs with Aunt Lulu."

"I know, Dad," Zoey said. "'Cause I need profits to buy more fabric."

"*Woof!*" agreed Draper before resting his head on his paws.

"Draper is a good business dog," Marcus said, stroking the dog's silky ears. "Aren't you, old boy?"

"As long as he gets paid in treats," Zoey said.

Draper stood up and waddled over to the treat tin.

They all laughed.

"He definitely knows *that* word," Mr. Webber

said, getting up to give Draper what he was so obviously expecting.

After the market research, the family settled on the family room sofa to relax and watch a movie. Draper padded in and stood in front of the coffee table, looking from Zoey to Marcus to Dad, his eyebrows quirking as if to ask where *he* was supposed to sit.

Zoey looked at her dad with pleading eyes.

"Can Draper come up on the sofa, Dad? *Pleeeease?*"

Draper wasn't usually allowed on the furniture. But Mr. Webber had a hard time resisting the puppy dog eyes being cast at him by both Draper *and* Zoey.

"Okay," he said. "But just for tonight as a special . . . T-R-E-A-T."

"Why are you spelling 'treat'?" Zoey asked.

Draper ran straight back into the kitchen.

"*That's* why," Marcus said, grinning. "Because Draper knows the T word."

"You better get up and give him one," said Mr. Webber. "Otherwise he's going to spend the entire movie whining under the treat tin."

Zoey went into the kitchen where, sure enough, Draper was sitting under the treat tin, gazing up at it worshipfully. As soon as Zoey had come in, his tail swept from side to side because he knew his prayer to the treat tin would soon be answered.

"This is your last one for tonight," Zoey said sternly as she gave him a treat. "Aunt Lulu said you're not supposed to have too many you-know-whats, and you've already had a bazillion today."

Draper trotted back into the family room at Zoey's heels, and Mr. Webber lifted him onto the sofa.

"Just this once, Draper," he said. "We're not going to make a habit of this."

Draper replied by giving him a wet lick on his face. Then he curled up between Mr. Webber and Zoey with a low grumble and closed his eyes. He'd worked hard enough for one day.

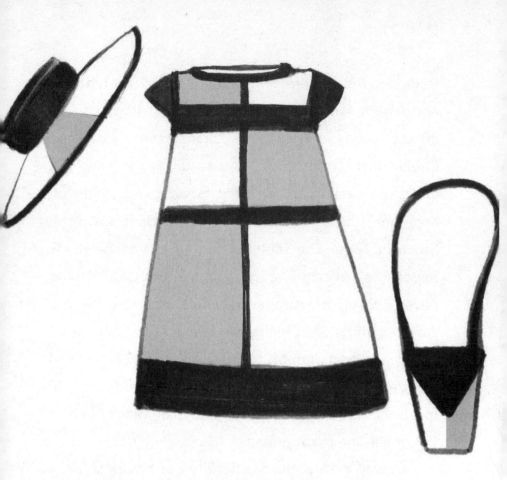

CHAPTER 3

Chic on the Cheap

Do you want a perfect example of why I need to make money to buy more fabric? So I can be chic on the cheap! I saw the most beautiful dress in *Très Chic*, and I wanted it so badly—until I saw how much it cost. I still *wanted* it after that, but I couldn't *afford* it. So,

I cut out the picture and stuck it in my sketchbook and I kept looking at it and wishing I had enough money to buy it. And then—*brain wave*—I realized I could make it instead! I had to go online and look in a store catalog to see what fabric it was made of, and then I asked Marcus if he could drive me to A Stitch in Time. The material turned out to be really expensive—to buy enough to make the dress would have used up practically my whole store credit—but Jan recommended a more reasonable substitute. That way, I had enough to buy notions to Zoeyfy it—I decided to add some extra colors to the trim and put in a bright blue zipper instead of a plain black one like the one in the magazine.

Anyway, being able to afford to get fabrics so I can keep being chic on the cheap is why I'm so excited to get my designer dog outfits business idea off the ground. But more on that in a later blog post!

No, not again! Zoey thought she'd *finally* gotten the zipper perfect on her version of the color-block dress she loved from *Très Chic*, but there was a little pucker right at the bottom. She'd have to do it over. She wanted the dress to be absolutely perfect, just the way it looked in the magazine, but she was getting tired. Her dad and Marcus had finished watching the movie and gone to sleep.

Draper gave a soft doggie snore from under the worktable. At least *he* wasn't frustrated. No, Draper seemed to be having a grand old time at the Webber Hotel, enjoying walkies, treats, and, of course, plenty of naps.

It took another half hour to redo the zipper, but it was worth the effort. Finally, after all her hard work, the dress looked almost exactly like the one in the picture she'd cut out of *Très Chic*. In fact, as she tried it on and stood in front of the mirror, Zoey thought she liked it even better, because of the little extra touches of color.

She really needed to start on her dog outfits business. Otherwise, what would happen if she saw another amazing dress she couldn't afford in *Très Chic*? She'd be totally stuck!

It was time to call in her team of advisers. Zoey sent a text to Kate and her other two friends, Priti

Holbrooke and Libby Flynn: **Need your advice about a project. Can we meet up?**

Priti was the first to respond. **Yes! Let's meet at the mall tomorrow. Then we can talk AND shop!** ☺

Sounds like a plan, Zoey texted. **Who can drive?**

My mom can, Libby volunteered. **We'll pick you up first, then Kate, then Priti. What time?**

12? Then we can get there right after the mall opens, Kate suggested.

See you then! Zoey texted.

Draper lifted his nose and looked up at Zoey expectantly as soon as she put down her phone.

"Yes, Draper. I've finished my dress and made plans for tomorrow. You're right. It's time for walkies."

The next day Zoey put on the color-block dress to wear to the mall. It made her feel good to be "put together" when she went shopping. Just after twelve, Mrs. Flynn arrived with Libby.

"Hi, Zoey," Mrs. Flynn said as Zoey got into the car. "Well, look at you—the two of you look like twins!"

Zoey couldn't believe her eyes—Libby was wearing the exact same dress as she was. Well, not exactly the same—because Libby's didn't have the extra touches of color Zoey had added to hers.

"That's the same dress that was in *Très Chic* this month, right?" Zoey asked.

"I can't remember," Libby said. She read *Très Chic* but not as avidly as Zoey. "Aunt Lexie sent it in her latest fashion care package from H. Cashin's."

"You're so lucky to have an aunt who works there." Zoey sighed. "I *love* that dress, but there was no way I could afford it. I made this one."

"You should be very proud of yourself," Libby's mom said. "You did a fantastic job. In fact, get out of the car, both of you. I want to take a picture of you together to send to Lexie."

"But, Mom—" Libby protested.

"Come on, it'll only take a minute," Mrs. Flynn said. "Hop to it!"

Libby slid out of the car, and she and Zoey stood side by side with their arms across each other's shoulders while Libby's mom took a few pictures with her cell phone.

"Come on, Mom. We're late to pick up Kate and Priti," Libby said.

"Okay, let's go," Mrs. Flynn said as she got back into the car after texting one of the pictures to her sister. "Lexie will get such a kick out of this."

As she backed out of the Webbers' driveway, she said, "I'm so glad you and Libby have become such good friends, Zoey. You're like two peas in a pod."

Libby glanced at Zoey. "Ignore all vegetable comparisons," she whispered.

Zoey giggled.

"I'm glad we're friends too," she told Mrs. Flynn. "Vegetable or no vegetable," she whispered to Libby, who smiled.

"How long do you think it'll take Kate and Priti to notice we're matching?" Libby asked.

"Twenty seconds?" Zoey guessed.

"I bet you it takes Kate at least ten seconds longer than Priti," Libby said.

When Kate opened the car door, Libby and Zoey started counting silently in their heads . . . *One Mississippi, two Mississippi* . . . Zoey was up to "thirty Mississippis" by the time Kate asked, "Wait, isn't Spirit Week over? No one told me it was a repeat of Twin Day."

"It's not," Zoey explained. "I just loved this dress when I saw it in *Très Chic*, but I couldn't afford it, so I made it instead."

"And my aunt who works at H. Cashin's sent it to me in one of her fashion care packages," Libby said.

"Wow," Kate said. "Did you know you were both going to wear them?"

"No!" Libby and Zoey said at the same time. "Jinx!" they said at the same time again. And they both laughed.

"You guys must be fashion psychics," Kate said.

"They both have good taste in dresses," said Mrs. Flynn.

"Now we have to see how long it takes Priti to notice," Zoey said. "It took you thirty seconds."

Priti's eyes widened as soon as she saw Zoey and Libby.

"Those dresses are fab! And you're so adorably twinish! I want one too!" she said. "Can you make me one, Zo?"

"Three seconds!" Libby said. "I win!"

Kate gave her a high five. Priti looked confused.

"Never mind. We were just trying to guess how long it would take for you to notice," Zoey told Priti. "You know, I'd love to make a dress for you, but it took me a long time to get this one right. And I have to get started on the *project*."

"Oh, that's right," Priti said. "The mystery project!"

"It won't be a mystery for long," Zoey said.

When Mrs. Flynn dropped off the girls at the mall, they headed straight up to the food court to get some snacks and settle down to business.

"When I walked Draper yesterday, people asked me if I could make outfits for their dogs," Zoey explained, showing them a photo of Draper in the outfit she had made for him. "It was actually Kate's idea to start a business."

"Not really," said Kate, who never liked to take credit for anything unless it was on the sports field.

"It was," said Zoey firmly. "But I couldn't fig-ure out how to do it until I heard Marcus talking at dinner about this website called Myfundmaker."

"Oh, I've heard of that site!" Priti exclaimed. "Sashi pledged to some music project. She got a free download of the CD when it was done."

"You can pledge at different levels," Zoey explained. "Because maybe not everyone has a dog, or even if they do, maybe they aren't the kind of people who like to dress up their dogs in cute outfits—"

"People like that exist?!" Libby exclaimed.

"Well, yeah," Kate said. "Can you imagine some tough Rottweiler guard dog in Draper's cute outfit?"

The girls all giggled at the thought of a group of guard dogs in Draper's outfit.

"Anyway," Zoey said, trying to steer the discussion back to the project, "what do you think?"

"I think it's a great idea," Libby said. "Count me in as a funder—I want an outfit for Chester!"

"I want to pledge, but we don't have a dog," Kate said.

"We did have a goldfish named Cheeto for a while, but no dogs." Priti sighed. "Maybe I can get my grandparents to buy one for their Basset Hound."

"That's why I need some cute rewards for people who want to contribute but don't have a dog," Zoey said. "Any brain waves?"

"What if we made cards with Draper's paw print on them?" Priti suggested, pointing her french fry for emphasis. "We could dip his paw in ink and get him to press on the card."

"Wouldn't that be a little cruel to Draper?" Libby asked. "It might hurt his paw."

"What if we just did one and then you drew the rest?" Kate suggested to Zoey.

"That could work," Zoey said. "It would be quicker, too!"

"But you need more swag for people who give bigger pledges," Priti pointed out. "How about for the next level they get a signed sketch of one of your designs?"

"And the next level could be the outfit in their dog's size—that's the one I want to do—and then you could have, like, a super-duper pledge reward for people who give a lot of money," Libby suggested. "They'd get everything—the Draper paw print, the signed sketch, and the dog outfit. Plus, you list their name as an official project sponsor on Sew Zoey."

"Ooh! I like that idea," Zoey said. "That might get my blog readers to pledge. And listing people as sponsors on Sew Zoey won't cost anything extra."

She smiled at her friends.

"You guys are the best brainstormers ever," she said. "I'm so happy you're as excited about this as I am."

"We want to help you keep making your awesome designs," Priti said, "because then you can keep making cool things for us! Wink, wink."

"Let's have some frozen yogurt to celebrate!" Libby said.

"I wish I had room," Zoey said. "I'm too full."

"Me too," Priti said. "I can't eat another bite."

"I can!" Kate declared. "Come on, Libby!"

When the other two were gone, Zoey asked Priti how things were going at home. A little while back, Priti had confided to Zoey that her parents were fighting a lot and were going to see a counselor.

She'd been freaking out about the possibility of them getting divorced.

"Things are a bit better now that they've started seeing the counselor," Priti said, but the smile faded from her face and her eyes. "At least you can tell they're really trying to be nicer to each other, even though they still end up bickering."

"Well, it hasn't been that long, right?" Zoey observed. "Dad says that problems only get solved overnight on TV."

"I guess," Priti said. "But I try not to think about it too much—because when I do, I start worrying and sometimes it's hard to stop."

"Hard to stop what?" Kate asked, sitting down with her frozen yogurt cone.

"Oh, nothing," Priti said.

Kate glanced from Zoey to Priti. "Is everything all right?"

Priti saw Libby walking toward them with her cup of frozen yogurt.

"I really don't want to talk about it now, okay?" she said.

"Okay, fine," Kate said, and the three friends

slipped into silence just as Libby got back to the table.

"What's going on?" Libby asked.

Silence.

"Um, well . . . ," Zoey started to speak.

"*Nothing*," Priti said. "Ready to shop till we drop?"

Zoey noticed Libby was a little quieter after lunch than she was before. But her head was so filled with all the ideas that her friends had given her for her project, it was hard to think about anything else. She was even having a hard time staying focused on shopping, and that was *very* unusual!

It was almost a relief when it was time to meet Mrs. Flynn for the ride home.

"So when should we wear our dresses to school together?" Libby asked. "I can't wait to be twinsies!"

"Me too! But I'm not sure when I'm going to get a chance to wash it," Zoey said. "I'll let you know soon."

"Okay!" Libby said.

Zoey thanked Mrs. Flynn for the ride and then burst through the front door of her house to a waggy-tailed, licky welcome from Draper.

"Come on, boy. We've got work to do!" she said, racing up the stairs to her room. "It's time to get this project page set up, so we can start selling your outfits!"

CHAPTER 4

Swirly Girls

My friends and I had a business brainstorming session in the food court at the mall last weekend. I think food helps you brainstorm better, don't you? I thought their fro-yo swirls were really pretty and figured it would be awesome to have a swirly dress, too. My friends

had great ideas for the rewards for the different levels
of pledges to my dogwear design project, which I'm
going to set up on Myfundmaker. I've started creating
the project page, but it isn't live yet because I need
Aunt Lulu's help to finish working out the financial
details and she's still away at her conference. But that
means I still have my business partner, Draper, here with
me, which I love. He's curled up, sleeping at my feet as
I write this, his warm chin heavy on my toes. How could
he sleep at a time like this? I don't think Draper is nearly
as excited about this project as I am!

"So have you thought about what you're going to do
for your Myfundmaker video yet?" Marcus asked.

Zoey was making herself an after-school snack
of apple slices and peanut butter. Draper was sitting by her feet, looking up at the counter hopefully.
Zoey knew what he wanted. She looked to make
sure her dad wasn't around and then let Draper lick
the peanut-butter-covered knife.

"What video?" she asked.

"The one for your project page," Marcus said.

"All the best-funded ones have a video that explains what the project is about to get people interested. Some are so awesome, you want to invest in the project just because of the video."

"Oh nooooo." Zoey groaned. "I didn't realize I had to do a video."

"Don't worry," Marcus said. "I can shoot it on my phone and edit it on my laptop. I haz the software."

"Really? You're the best!" Zoey said, her face brightening. "Super Brother to the rescue!"

"Yeah, yeah, I know." Marcus grinned. "So what do you have in mind?"

Zoey munched on her apple slice. "How about I dress Draper in his outfit, and then we take a video of him out in the yard," she suggested. "I can encourage him to perform with some T-R-E-A-T-S."

She was careful to spell the word "treats," so Draper didn't make a beeline for the treat tin. Again.

"Good idea," Marcus said. "And then you can take him for W-A-L-K-I-E-S, and I can film you around the neighborhood."

"Sounds like a P-L-A-N!" Zoey said. "Oh, wait.

Draper doesn't know that word! Meet back here in five?"

"Perfecto!"

Zoey finished the last of her apple slices and headed upstairs to get Draper's outfit. Draper followed close behind, his tail wagging wildly. When they returned to the kitchen, Marcus was already there, putting Zoey's dish in the dishwasher. "Wow! You're doing my dishes?" Zoey asked.

"Just this once," Marcus teased. "Don't get used to it. Wanna get Draper in his outfit while I finish cleaning up?"

Draper's tail kept wagging and wagging . . . until Zoey tried to put the outfit on him. Then it drooped, and Draper squirmed in Zoey's arms.

"What, you don't like Zoey's clothes?" Marcus asked. "What kind of spokesdog are you, Draper?"

"He's the best spokesdog ever!" Zoey said, trying again to put the outfit on the not-particularly-cooperative dog. "Because good spokesdogs get lots of . . . treats!"

As soon as he heard the word "treats," Draper stood at attention, allowing Zoey to finish buttoning the outfit. Then he trotted over to the counter where the treat tin stood and pointed his nose in the air.

Marcus laughed. "Draper is definitely Pavlov's dog," he said.

"Who's Pablo?" Zoey asked.

"Not Pablo. Pavlov. He was a Russian guy who did these experiments about dogs and how they're conditioned to respond to things. Like when you say the T word, Draper is conditioned to go over to where he knows the T-R-E-A-T tin is located."

"That's not conditioning. That's just because Draper's brilliant. Right, best spokesdog ever?" Zoey crooned, scratching behind Draper's ears. He wagged his tail and barked in the direction of the treat tin.

"I'll give you one now, but you have to perform for the camera before you get the rest," Zoey said, giving him a treat and putting some extras in her pocket.

Marcus and Zoey went out into the backyard, followed by Draper, whose nose was trained in the direction of Zoey's pocket.

"Okay, I'll stand over here," Marcus said, walking across the yard so he wasn't shooting into the sun. "You get him to run toward the camera."

Zoey moved to just behind Marcus's left shoulder.

"Come here, Draper!" she called to the dog, who was sniffing the base of an ornamental maple tree.

He turned to look at her, but didn't come. Instead, he lifted his leg and relieved himself.

Marcus started laughing.

"Best spokesdog ever!" he said. "Right."

"You better edit that out," Zoey warned him.

"Don't worry. I will," Marcus promised.

"Draper! Here, boy!" Zoey called again.

Draper started ambling slowly in Zoey's direction.

"Can you get him to look a little more enthusiastic?" Marcus asked. "He looks like he's half asleep!"

"He's *old*!" Zoey protested. Still, she reached into her pocket for a treat and held it out to Draper on the palm of her hand. "C'mon, boy! Treat!"

As soon as he heard the magic word, Draper's ears pricked up, and he switched gears from amble to lumber. Zoey encouraged him to move even faster by repeating the T word over and over. By the time Draper reached her, he'd almost made it to a trot.

"Good boy!" Zoey told him, giving him the treat.

"I wouldn't exactly call that 'frolicking,' but it's probably the best we're going to get from an old boy like Draper," Marcus said.

They repeated the exercise a few more times, so Marcus could get additional footage. But once Draper realized Zoey had run out of treats, he lost all interest in the proceedings and flopped down onto the grass in protest.

Marcus reviewed the video he had. "It's okay. I think we've got enough of this," he said.

Zoey, who was looking over Marcus's shoulder at his phone's screen, started laughing.

"Look at him! He's so cute with his ears bouncing."

"I know." Marcus walked over and patted

Draper's head. "Come on. Let's get him leashed up and take him for walkies, so I can get some footage of that."

Draper perked up when he heard "walkies," another of his magic words. He didn't jump up—the arthritis in his poor old legs made it too hard for him to do that—but Zoey knew if he could have jumped, he would have. Instead, he struggled to his feet, ungainly but dignified.

Zoey went inside to get his leash from the counter and then hooked it up to his collar.

"Okay, Draper. Let's go and show off your outfit to the neighborhood!" she said.

Marcus walked ahead of them backward, filming them walking down the street. Zoey made sure to tell Marcus when he was about to bump into someone's mailbox or trip over a dip in a driveway. As if on cue, someone approached, walking an Italian greyhound.

"I love your dog's outfit," she said. "Where did you get it? Roxy would look adorable in that."

"I made it," Zoey said.

"Seriously? You should start a business," the

dog owner said. "I bet you could sell a lot of those. Just precious."

"Funny you should say that," Marcus said, keeping the camera rolling. "Check out Zoey's Myfundmaker page—she's launching a project to sell them."

"Great!" the dog owner exclaimed. "What's the name of your project?"

"Um . . . ," Zoey said, looking at Marcus in a panic. She hadn't gotten around to thinking of a catchy name yet.

"Doggie Duds!" he said without missing a beat.

"I'll be sure to look out for it," the dog owner said. "Roxy *definitely* wants one of those outfits. Don't you, Rox?"

Roxy, who had been sniffing around the back of Draper's outfit, looked up and wagged her tail.

"See? She does! We'll be looking for your Doggie Duds online!" the owner said as she walked off with her dog.

Marcus pressed pause on the video and gave Zoey a high five.

"Wow. We couldn't have paid someone to be a better advertisement!" he said.

"How did you come up with that name on the spur of the moment?" Zoey asked. "My mind was a total blank!"

"What can I say? Pure genius," Marcus said.

"Okay, don't get too carried away," Zoey said. "Otherwise your head won't fit back through the front door."

"Speaking of which, that's where we should go. Back through the front door. I want to do a little 'What was your inspiration for this project?' interview with you, and my director's vision tells me it should be at your worktable," Marcus explained.

Zoey understood creative vision, but she couldn't help teasing her brother. "Where's your director's chair?"

"Ha, ha, ha," Marcus said. "We'll see how hard you're laughing when my awesome video gets your project funded. Come on, we have Oscar-worthy work to do!"

Marcus had Zoey sit at her sewing table, making sure that her dressmaker's dummy, Marie Antoinette, was visible behind her. Then he experimented by moving the light around until he was satisfied.

"Okay, here we go," Marcus said. "Doggie Duds interview, take one. What was your inspiration?"

"Well, I guess the inspiration was my aunt's dog, Draper, who stays with us when she travels on business. He was keeping me company while I was designing people clothes, and I decided I should design him something too."

"Some duds of his own?" Marcus asked.

"That's right. And then when we went out for a walk, people starting asking me where I bought Draper's outfit, because they wanted to buy one for their dog."

"Leading to the creation of the Doggie Duds project."

Being interviewed by Marcus was actually kind of fun, Zoey thought. Because he was her brother, she wasn't nervous, not the way she was when she was on *Fashion Showdown* or when she was interviewed for the online version of *Très Chic*. It was just like hanging out and chatting with Marcus, except he was filming her with his phone.

"That was fun," she told him when they finished. "Seriously, thanks, Marcus. It's really great of you to do this."

"Anything to help my little sis launch her mega-empire. It was fun for me too. Just promise you'll let me do all the music for your runway shows when you're some famous fashion mogul."

"It's a deal!" Zoey said. "Wouldn't that be amazing?"

Draper came over and put his head on Marcus's knee.

"Draper wants in on this deal," Marcus said. "He says he wants five percent of the profits, payable in dog T-R-E-A-T-S, for being the inspiration and spokesdog."

"That's pretty steep," Zoey said. "I need money to buy fabric."

"Draper drives a tough bargain," Marcus said, petting Draper's ears, "but maybe I can convince him to negotiate."

They were still laughing and negotiating over Draper's cut when Mr. Webber came home for dinner.

"Do you want to come over for a sleepover on Saturday?" Kate asked Zoey on the bus the next morning. "We haven't had one in a while. Priti already said she can come."

"Sure," Zoey said. "I just have to check with Dad tonight."

That night at dinner, when she asked her dad about the sleepover, he said, "Sure. Actually, that will work out well."

"What do you mean 'work out well'?" Zoey asked.

Her father fidgeted with his fork and then put it down resolutely.

"There's something I've been wanting to discuss with you both," he said.

Zoey and Marcus gave each other a *What's this all about* look.

"You know how much I loved . . . will always love . . . Mom, right?" Dad asked them.

"Yeah . . . ," Marcus said.

Zoey just nodded, wondering where he was going with this.

"It's been ten years since she passed, and . . . to be honest, I've always been too busy looking after you guys and working to even think about it." He took a deep breath. "But someone at work has a friend he thinks I'd really get along well with so . . . he set me up on a, you know, date."

Wait. Dad is going on a DATE?

"Look, I know you might have some, you know, feelings about this, so you can ask me any questions you want," Dad said. "And it's just a date. I'm rusty at this stuff, so it's not like I'm going to be rushing into anything."

Zoey definitely had feelings. Shock was the first one. Dad had never dated, *ever*. Did this mean she was going to end up with a stepmom? She liked things the way they were, just her, Dad, and Marcus. How would it be to add another person in the house? Stepmothers were always evil in fairy tales. Zoey knew those were just fairy tales, but still . . .

She needed to know more about this . . . lady.

"What's her name?" Zoey asked.

"Cara Richards."

"Does she have kids?" Marcus asked.

Zoey hadn't even thought of that. What if her dad married this Cara Richards lady, and she ended up with stepsisters and they had to share a room and she had to get rid of her workspace? Even worse, what if the stepsibling turned out to be someone like *Ivy Wallace*, the meanest girl at Mapleton Prep?

"She has a son and a daughter," Dad said. "I think the son is a year or two younger than you, Marcus, and the daughter is the same age as Zoey."

Zoey had a vision of her worktable and Marie Antoinette being carried out of her room to make space for a future stepsister's bed. It was a vision she didn't like at all.

But then she remembered how many times Dad had seemed sad when he came home from parents' night, because he was there by himself. How she'd overheard him talking to Aunt Lulu once about how lonely it felt being a single dad. As much as Zoey didn't want things to change, she didn't want her dad to be lonely.

"Where are you going to take her?" Zoey asked.

"I don't know. I was thinking about the Jukebox," Dad said. "The food is good, and it's not too loud, so you can actually have a conversation. What do you think?"

"It's okay," Zoey said. "But it's not really datey. You should take her to that place with the fish tank. . . . What's it called?"

"Aquaterra," Marcus said. "Yeah, that place is much more date-worthy."

"Good idea," Dad said. "Like I said, it's been a while since I've done this."

He looked at Marcus, then at Zoey. "Are you sure you're okay with this?"

"I guess," Marcus said.

Zoey shrugged and nodded.

But as she went upstairs to her room after dinner, she still wasn't sure if she wanted Dad's date to go well so he'd be happier, or for him to have total date fail so that everything in her life could stay exactly the way it was.

CHAPTER 5

No *Pup*arazzi

Some entrepreneur I am! I didn't even realize that all the most successful projects have videos to explain what they're about and to get pledgers interested. But luckily for me, Marcus a.k.a. The Best Brother in the World (and he didn't even pay me to say that!) not only told me about it, but also offered to shoot and edit the video for me. He's just *sooooooo* awesome. (Okay, he might have paid me to add the last part. J/k!)

Draper is the star of the campaign, which makes sense because he was the inspiration for Doggie Duds. That's the name of the project; again thanks to brilliant and witty (!!) Marcus, who thought of it on the spur of the moment when my mind was a total blank. In honor of Draper's stardom, I designed him a red carpet outfit. I can't wait to earn enough money to make it. We'll have to call him Dapper Draper.

I'm really excited to launch the Myfundmaker campaign, but I'm also nervous. I've got mixed feelings about some other stuff too. Things might be changing around here. I know change doesn't mean bad; sometimes change can be for the better, like when Ms. Austen started as the new head at Mapleton Prep and we didn't have to wear uniforms anymore. But what happens if they change for the worse?

When Mr. Webber came downstairs dressed for his date on Saturday night, Zoey was horrified.

"You're wearing *that*?" she exclaimed.

Her father looked down at the crumpled pants, polo shirt, and sweater he had on.

"What's the matter with what I'm wearing?" he asked, looking confused.

Zoey shook her head.

"Dad, *Dad* . . . this is what happens when all you watch is sports," she said. "You can't go out on a date in *that*. Especially a *first* date."

"Are you going to tell me what I *am* supposed to wear?" Dad asked.

"Come on," Zoey said, heading for the stairs. "It's time for the Webber version of *Fashion Police*, starring Jack and Zoey Webber."

"Now I'm *really* nervous," her father said.

"You should be more nervous about showing up on a date dressed like *that*," Zoey said. "I haven't ever been on a date, but even I know you have to dress to impress."

Mr. Webber laughed. "Okay, Fashion Police. Sentence me to a better outfit."

Zoey went into her dad's closet and picked out a pair of dark jeans, a crisp oxford shirt, a tweed jacket, and a pair of polished loafers.

Her dad went into the bathroom to change, and when he came out, he gave a little twirl. "What's the verdict, Officer?"

"So much better!" Zoey exclaimed. "Now you look like a cool dad instead of a dork dad."

Her dad looked at himself in the mirror that hung on the inside of the closet door.

"You know what? I feel cooler too," he said. He came and sat on the bed next to Zoey. "Zo, I'm really nervous about tonight. It's been so long, I think I've forgotten how to do the whole dating thing."

"You'll be fine, Dad," Zoey said, giving him a hug. "Just remember what you always tell me—be yourself, and she's sure to like you."

"I give good advice, don't I?" her dad said. "Maybe I should start listening to myself." He held her hand. "Listen, Zo, are you sure you're okay with this? You know, me going out on a date?"

"I guess," Zoey said. "I mean, I sort of have mixed feelings about it."

"I sort of have mixed feelings about it too," he said. "Let's just see how it goes. It's only dinner."

"But what if you really like her and then you get married and I have a stepsister and we have to share a room and I don't have any room for Marie Antoinette and my sewing machine and—" Zoey blurted.

"Whoa there, honey, let's not get ahead of ourselves here. Even if I think this lady is the bee's knees, I won't rush into anything," Dad said, patting Zoey's leg for reassurance. "Remember, you and Marcus are still my number-one priority. Okay?"

"Okay," Zoey said. "Have a good time, Dad. And try not to tell too many *corny* jokes."

Mr. Webber laughed. "Got it. I'll only tell asparagus-y jokes. Okay?"

Priti was already over at the Mackey house when Zoey walked over there for the sleepover. Zoey had gone excavating for fashion treasures in Kate's closet and found a beading set Kate had asked for in a rare display of interest in something other than sports gear. Except it had been gathering dust in the closet ever since Mrs. Mackey bought it, and Kate's mom kept nagging her to do some beading.

"Look at all these amazing beads!" Priti exclaimed. "I can't believe this has just been sitting in your closet! We have to make something."

"Stop, you sound just like Mom!" Kate groaned.

"It would be fun to make something," Zoey said, eyeing the beads longingly. She touched the sticks and stones bracelet on her wrist, the one from her fashion fairy godmother, Fashionsista.

"What if we made matching BFF bracelets? We could pick beads that represent each of us and create a pattern," Kate suggested.

"I love it!" Priti exclaimed.

"It's a miracle," Kate said. "You've managed to get me excited about beading!"

Zoey laughed. "Let's choose our colors before you lose steam," she said.

"I pick gold," Kate said, "because someday I want to win a gold medal in the Olympics."

Priti surveyed the selection of beads. "This one is perfect for me," she said, picking up a rose gold one. "Because it's got bling, but the rose color is warm and sunny."

Kate and Zoey laughed.

"You're right," Zoey said. "That *is* perfect for you!"

She stared at the box of beads.

"Now the question is . . . which one is perfect for me?"

One color after the other seemed to call to Zoey, each for its own reason. It was impossible to choose.

"How about this one?" Kate suggested, picking up a twinkly, silvery bead. "Because it's kind of starry, and you're becoming a fashion star."

"And you're going to be an even bigger one someday," Priti said.

Suddenly, the twinkly, silvery bead seemed like the absolutely perfect one for Zoey.

"That's it!" she said. "Now we have to work out a pattern."

They each laid out the pattern of beads on a tray and then got to work making the bracelets.

"So how's the dog clothing project coming along?" Kate asked. "Do you know when it will be ready?"

"Hopefully in the next two weeks," Zoey said. "Marcus is making me a video for the campaign page. He filmed it the other day, and he's going to edit it for me."

"That's *so* nice," Priti said. "I can't imagine Tara or Sashi doing that for me. Tara's always studying and Sashi's always practicing."

"It *is* really nice of him," Zoey said. "I have to admit, when it comes to brothers, Marcus rates pretty high."

"What else do you have to do after the video is done?" Kate asked.

"Wait till Aunt Lulu gets back to help me work out the business plan," Zoey said. "Dad can help me, but he says Aunt Lulu is really the expert."

"And then . . . ," Priti prompted.

"And then we launch!" Zoey said.

"I can't wait," Kate said. "Mom already talked about it to some of the soccer moms, and they love the idea."

Zoey couldn't wait either. But Dad was firm about making sure they had the business plan all figured out before the page went live.

When the girls finished their bracelets, they put them on and went downstairs to watch a movie.

Mrs. Mackey made them brownies as a special treat, because she was so happy they'd finally used the beading kit!

When Zoey got home the next morning, the house seemed oddly quiet. She realized she'd become used to the padding and scraping of Draper's paws on the hardwood floor as he scampered to the front door to welcome her whenever she came through it.

"Draper!" she called. "Come here, boy! I'm home!"

But there was no sign of the faithful pooch. *He's probably going for walkies with Marcus,* Zoey figured. *Lucky dog!*

"Hi, honey!" her dad called from upstairs. "I just got out of the shower. I'll come say hi in a bit."

Zoey went up to her room to check her blog and work on her project page. Her dad had set it up but thought she should write the descriptions. She looked at the more successful projects and tried to figure out what it was about their pages that got people interested. Was it a great video? Was it a cute message? Did it have really cool rewards for each level of giving? Or was it the project itself?

She was busy writing her project description when her father knocked on the door and then came into her bedroom.

"Hi, honey. How was the sleepover?"

"It was fun! We made friendship bracelets." She held out her arm to show her dad. "See?"

"Very pretty," Mr. Webber said, taking a seat at the end of the bed.

"How was your date?" Zoey asked.

"It was"—her dad hesitated—"good."

"You don't sound very sure about that."

"No, I had a nice time. Cara is a great lady—smart, pretty, interesting to talk to. . . . She even laughed at my jokes," he said.

"Nobody's perfect," Zoey said.

"Ha-ha, very funny," her dad said. "She also complimented me on my jacket."

"Oh, well, she has good taste in clothes," Zoey said.

"Listen, Zo, I've got something difficult I need to tell you."

He sounded and looked *very* serious all of a sudden. Zoey started worrying about the difficult things he could need to tell her. Did Ms. Austen call to say she was in trouble? Or wait—maybe her dad had fallen head over heels in love with that Cara lady and married her on the first date, and she already had an evil stepmonster she'd never even met! "Did you marry that Cara lady?"

"What? No! Where did you get that idea?" exclaimed Mr. Webber. "She's really a lovely person, but . . ."

"But?"

"There wasn't any special connection—not the kind I had with your mom the first time we went out."

Her father looked sad, and Zoey leaned over and put her head on his shoulder. He planted a kiss into her hair and put his arm around her.

"Zoey . . . last night while I was out with Cara, Marcus was watching TV with Draper. Draper seemed fine. Marcus went up to his room to work on the video for your project for a while, but when he came back down an hour or so later, Draper hadn't moved an inch," Dad said. "Marcus didn't want to bother me while I was out, so he called the vet. The vet said to take Draper straight to the emergency animal hospital, so Marcus did."

"Is Draper okay?" Zoey asked, suddenly overcome with dread.

"I saw the note from Marcus when I got home and rushed to the animal hospital. I got there in time to see Draper and say good-bye, but . . . I'm sorry, Zo, he's gone."

"What? But I didn't even get to say good-bye to him!" Zoey exclaimed, bursting into tears.

"I know, honey. I know," her dad said, holding her while she cried. "It's never easy to lose someone you love, whether it's a person or a pet."

"It's all my fault," Zoey wailed. "If Marcus wasn't working on my stupid video, then he'd have been with Draper and Draper would be okay."

"No, Zoey, that's not true. It's not anyone's fault. Draper was fourteen years old, that's . . . How old is that in dog years?"

Zoey did the math in her head. "N-ninety-eight," she muttered with a sniff.

"The vet said he didn't suffer. He was an old dog who'd had a good life, surrounded by people he loved," Mr. Webber said.

"I guess," Zoey said. "But I still wish I'd been able to say good-bye to him."

"I know, honey," her dad said. "I expect Aunt Lulu will feel that way too."

Poor Aunt Lulu. She doted on Draper like he was her child.

"Did you tell her yet?" Zoey asked.

"I'm going to wait until later this afternoon, when the conference is over. It's important for Lulu's business, and there's no point upsetting her till then," he said. "She can't do anything for him now."

He sighed. "Your brother is really torn up. I remember when Lulu brought Draper home from the rescue place. He was the cutest little puppy, and Marcus had just started crawling a few months before." Zoey saw her father's eyes grow moist even though he smiled at the memory. "Marcus and Draper used to romp together on the floor like two little puppies. They were inseparable."

As bad as Zoey felt about not being there to say good-bye to Draper, she could only imagine how scary it must have been for Marcus to have to take him to the pet hospital all by himself.

Mr. Webber hugged Zoey again and then got up. "I have to go grocery shopping or we won't have anything to eat for the rest of the week. Call me if you need anything or if you want to talk, okay?"

Zoey nodded.

As soon as he left, Zoey felt at a loss. She didn't have the heart to work on any sewing—especially any dog outfits. She thought about writing a blog post about Draper, but then she realized they hadn't told Aunt Lulu yet. The last thing she wanted was for her aunt to find out that her beloved dog had died by reading it on Sew Zoey.

Instead, Zoey got up and went to find Marcus. He wasn't in his room. But as soon as she got down to the kitchen, she could tell from the crash of cymbals and the back beat of the snare that he was down in the basement. She got some cookies for Marcus—and herself—and headed down to join him.

As soon as he saw her, he stopped playing. "Hey . . . did Dad . . . ?"

"He did," Zoey said, nodding sadly. "Do you want a cookie?"

"Yes, please." Marcus took a cookie from the plate. "The house feels so empty without Draper, doesn't it?"

"I know. It felt weird as soon as I got home, before I even knew anything, because he didn't come to greet me at the door."

"I hope Aunt Lulu isn't mad at me," Marcus said. "I wouldn't have left him alone if I thought something was wrong with him. Honest."

"It's not your fault, Marcus. Dad told me what the vet said," Zoey reassured him. "It's because Draper was an old dog. It was just his time to go."

"I know. But why did it have to happen when Aunt Lulu was away and when I was the only one home?"

Zoey shrugged. "Bad luck?"

"The worst luck in the entire universe," Marcus said.

"Seriously, don't worry about Aunt Lulu. She

knows how much you love—I mean, loved—Draper," Zoey said.

"I hope you're right." Marcus sighed, picking up his drumsticks. "Now if you don't want to get a headache, run upstairs. I'm having myself some serious drum therapy down here, and it's going to get real loud."

Mr. Webber returned with the groceries, and they were all in the kitchen unpacking when Aunt Lulu called to say she was done with her conference and about to leave the hotel for the airport. Marcus and Zoey stood silent and tense as their father, as gently as he could, broke the news of Draper's passing to their aunt over the phone.

"I'm so sorry, Lulu," he finished. "We're all devastated, especially the kids. . . . What? Sure, hold on."

He pushed the speakerphone.

"Aunt Lulu wants to talk to you guys," he said.

Zoey heard her aunt's voice, sounding kind of tearful, but . . . "Zo and Marcus, thank you both for taking such great care of Draper. I know you loved him as much as I did, and he always loved to spend time with you."

A lump formed in Zoey's throat.

"We loved having him here, Aunt Lulu," she managed to say. "The house feels empty without him."

"I know, honey," Aunt Lulu said. "And I know that he was an old boy and that every time I went away, there was a risk his time might come when I wasn't around to be with him. I'm just glad we had so many happy years with him and he had such a wonderful, loving home. Actually, two wonderful loving homes. Draper was doubly lucky, wasn't he?"

"Definitely," Marcus agreed.

"I'd better get to the airport," Aunt Lulu said. "I'm looking forward to coming home and hugging you all."

Zoey was relieved that Aunt Lulu seemed to take it so well. But missing Draper was a dull, heavy ache that hung over Zoey like a storm cloud.

She went up to her room and sat at her work-table, hoping she'd be inspired to sew something.

Maybe sewing therapy would work as well as drum therapy. But it just reminded her of how much she missed Draper's warm body curled up beneath her feet, his wet muzzle tickling her toes while she pressed the foot pedal of the machine.

Instead, she grabbed her sketchbook and pencil and curled up on her bed. The empty page made her feel even lonelier, but then an image of Draper came into her mind and she started sketching furiously. Soon, the page was filled with new dog-inspired designs.

CHAPTER 6

As the Saying Goes: All Dogs Go to Heaven ☹

I usually like to share good news with my Sew Zoey readers, but today is different. Something awful happened over the weekend—my aunt Lulu's dog, Draper, passed away. I've never lost a pet before, and even though Draper wasn't really *my* pet, he's been a part of the family for as a long as I can remember—since before I was even born as a matter of fact! It's so hard to imagine life without him. Last night, I thought I heard his tail thumping under the worktable when Dad came in to tell me to turn off the light. I was busy designing some new dog outfits, inspired by the thought of Draper making a beeline for the nearest treat jar. The one above is my favorite.

It seems so unfair that just when I'm so close to getting the Doggie Duds project launched, Draper, the one who inspired the idea, won't be here to see it happen. I mean, I knew he was an old dog, but he seemed fine, other than not exactly being the fastest runner you've ever seen. But he was ninety-eight in dog years, so it's not like you could expect him to be winning Olympic gold, even if the medal was made of treats!

Getting back to the school routine the next day wasn't enough to distract Zoey from her thoughts of Draper and the hollow feeling inside she had from his absence. When she met her friends for lunch in the cafeteria, she confessed how sad she was.

"I just can't stop missing him," she said. "It's not like I used to see him every day, even. But I knew he was there. And now I'm never going to be able to see him ever again."

"I wish I could say I knew how you feel," Priti said, "but the only pet we've ever had was Cheeto the goldfish, and all we did was say our good-byes when Mom flushed him down the toilet. It was sad, but not Draper sad. My grandparents have a Basset Hound, but they live far away."

"I've never had any kind of pet," Kate explained to Libby. "Not even a goldfish. It's too much responsibility."

Libby had a dog, though, so she had a deeper understanding of Zoey's grief. "I can't imagine what I'd do if we lost Chester. He's part of the family. He's only five, so hopefully it won't be for a long time. I don't even want to think about it."

She reached out to squeeze Zoey's hand and noticed the BFF bracelet on her wrist. "That's a cute bracelet. Is that new?"

Zoey felt her cheeks flushing, and she tried not

to look at Priti and Kate, who were wearing their bracelets too. She felt so awkward. Why hadn't they thought to make one for Libby? "Um . . . yeah. I . . . we . . ."

Priti moved her arm, as if trying to hide it under the table, and Libby noticed she was wearing a matching bracelet. And then she saw that Kate had one too.

"Oh . . . ," she said. "You've all got matching ones."

Silence. All there was at their table was awkward, uncomfortable silence, despite the surrounding clamor of the cafeteria.

"They're BFF bracelets," Kate confessed finally.

"We made them at the sleepover," Priti added.

"What sleepover?" Libby asked quietly.

Zoey wished then that she'd asked Kate to invite Libby to the sleepover. "The one at Kate's house," she said, feeling really bad about the fact that Libby had been excluded.

"I was going to invite you, but you were out of town," Kate explained.

"We each picked beads to represent us," Priti

said. "Kate is gold because she wants to win Olympic gold, Zoey is sparkly silver because she's a fashion star, and I'm rose gold because it's blingy and warm."

"Cool," said Libby.

But to Zoey she seemed subdued, and a minute later she said she had to get going, even though there were still five minutes left in the lunch period. Zoey felt terrible. She didn't want to force her new BFF on her old BFFs. But wouldn't it be great if they could all be BFFs together? She decided that when the time was right, she would talk to Kate and Priti about making a bracelet for Libby, too.

Between missing Draper and feeling bad about Libby, Zoey was miserable when she got home. She flopped onto her bed, staring up at the ceiling and wishing like anything that she could turn back time to before the sleepover, when Draper was still alive and she could remember to make Libby a BFF bracelet so Libby wouldn't feel left out.

Sadly, she couldn't do either of those things. But maybe what she *could* do was make something nice to cheer up her aunt. Sometimes sewing was a pick-me-up for Zoey when she was feeling down, and making things for people she loved was even better.

Zoey sat at her worktable with her sketchbook and picked up a pencil, trying to think of something really special to make Lulu. Her aunt already had lots of really great clothes, and now that Draper was gone, Zoey couldn't make more dog outfits—that thought made Zoey feel sad all over again. Suddenly, Zoey remembered her aunt talking about the ballroom dance lessons she'd been taking recently and how much fun they were. Aunt Lulu really loved the merengue and the waltz, even though she said the waltz made her dizzy if she didn't focus on her partner's face. Zoey decided to make her aunt a flowing skirt like she'd seen some of the contestants wear on the dance reality shows they watched together. She sketched a few different designs until she came up with the one that seemed to scream Aunt Lulu. Zoey wanted to get a silk-chiffon fabric that would swish and swirl around her aunt's ankles as she danced. But there was one big problem: Silk chiffon wasn't cheap.

Zoey rummaged in her bedside table and found the receipt from her last purchase at A Stitch in Time, so she could check the credit balance left from the Avalon competition. It was dwindling fast. She really needed to get Doggie Duds off the ground, and soon, or her sewing days would be through.

But in the meantime she needed a ride to the fabric store to pick up the chiffon and look for Doggie Duds inspiration.

"Marcus?" she called, heading toward her brother's room.

He didn't answer. She went to his door and peeped in. He was doing homework with his headphones on, his head bobbing up and down to the beat. No wonder he didn't hear her.

"Yo, *hermano!*" she said, tapping him on the back.

"*Si?*" he said, taking off his headphones.

"Can you drive me to A Stitch in Time? I want to make a present for Aunt Lulu to cheer her up."

"Yeah, okay. I could use a study break," Marcus said. "What are you going to make?"

"A skirt for ballroom dancing," Zoey said.

"*Bueno.* Hey, did she tell you about dancing with the guy who kept stepping on her toes?"

Zoey laughed. "No! What did she say?"

"Apparently, the instructor said they weren't allowed to look down at their feet; they had to look into each other's eyes," Marcus explained. "Well, the guy was so mesmerized by Aunt Lulu's eyes—or at least that's what she said—that he kept stepping on her feet. She had to ice her toes after class!"

Zoey knew how Aunt Lulu felt. She'd spent ages daydreaming about dancing with Lorenzo Romy, but when she finally did, he was a toe stepper too. And he didn't even say anything about being mesmerized with her eyes. He was just a bad dancer.

Walking through the doors of A Stitch in Time always gave Zoey a thrill. It was an Aladdin's cave of treasures for a creative girl with designer ambitions.

"Hi, Zoey!" called Jan, A Stitch in Time's friendly and knowledgeable owner, who'd popped her head out from the expensive fabrics aisle, where she was helping another customer. "I'll be with you soon if you need help. You just hang tight, okay?"

"Thanks, Jan," Zoey said, taking a shopping basket for her purchases and heading for the notions aisle. She wanted to get some cute buttons for her Doggie Duds designs. But after her dad's talk about sales and costs and making profits, she knew she had to be careful to pick cute but not-too-expensive buttons or else she wouldn't make enough money on the outfits.

A set of blue buttons with gold anchors gave her an idea for a nautical-themed version of the doggie outfit, and she found several sets of plastic buttons in bright colors to play around with. Zoey also found some cool wooden buttons for a more rustic, outdoorsy look she thought would be perfect for bigger, sporting dogs, like Lucky, the Labrador who lived down the street—assuming his owners decided to support Doggie Duds. She'd just have to make the outfits so cute that *everyone* would want them.

"So, what can I do for you, Miss Zoey?" Jan asked, interrupting her designing musings.

Zoey told Jan the sad news about Draper and

showed her the sketch of the skirt she wanted to make for Aunt Lulu to cheer her up.

"I was really hoping to make it out of silk chiffon, but I'm not sure I'm going to have enough money to buy that, and the lining and the zipper and these buttons. Plus, I have to buy some fabric for the Doggie Duds business I'm launching."

"Yes, I read about that on Sew Zoey," Jan exclaimed. "So exciting!" She took off her glasses and led the way to the expensive fabrics aisle, walking straight up to a beautiful silk chiffon that shimmered in the light. "This is sparkle chiffon, and it's one of my favorite fabrics! It's not cheap, but because you and your aunt Lulu are good customers, and I'm so sad to hear about Draper, I'll give you a deal. Do you think this is *the one* for your aunt's skirt?"

"I do!" Zoey exclaimed, letting the soft fabric float over her fingers. "It's absolutely perfect!"

Jan took down the bolt of fabric and went to put it on the counter. She helped Zoey pick out a solid, more economical chiffon for the lining, since it would be the side that wouldn't be seen.

"Now, about the fabrics for your dog business," Jan said. "I know your budget's tight. I've got a fifty-percent-off sale on the remnants. Look through to see if there's anything that would work."

"Great," Zoey said.

Jan spotted someone walking in the door. "See what you can find while I help this customer."

Zoey took the shopping basket over to the remnants bin, where Jan threw the tail ends of fabric bolts that weren't big enough to sell, or fabric that had accidentally been cut to the wrong length. She found some great bits of fabric that were too small to make much for a human but were perfect for dogs' clothes. Zoey's basket was full by the time she walked back to the counter.

"You've done well," Jan said, smiling.

"Can you add it up for me?" Zoey said. "I have to make sure I have enough credit left first."

"You should be okay," Jan said. "Let's cut the fabric for your aunt's skirt first."

After Jan measured and cut the chiffon with her sharp shears, Zoey watched anxiously as she rang up the purchases, hoping that there was enough credit left to cover everything. It was getting very close.

"Now for your special customer discount . . . ," Jan said, taking off another 10 percent.

When she saw the total, Zoey breathed a sigh of relief. She had just enough to buy everything, and even had two dollars credit left over.

"Thank you so much for the special customer discount," she said. "I couldn't have afforded it all without it."

Jan smiled. "When you're a hot fashion designer, I'll expect a special customer discount on my original Zoey Webber couture dress."

"Absolutely," Zoey said. "You're the best, Jan."

She took her bags of fabric and notions and went to find Marcus, who was waiting for her at the coffee shop. He'd brought his laptop with him, and when Zoey walked up, he had on his headphones and was working very intently on what she thought was his homework. But as soon as he saw her, he gestured her to come over and pulled off the headphones.

"Hey, Zo," he said. "Check this out."

Zoey put down her bags and pulled up the chair next to him.

"Here, put these on," he said, giving her the headphones and pressing play on the video.

On the screen, Draper rambled across the grass in the backyard, his tail wagging from side to side. Soft music played in the background, and then a voice Zoey recognized as belonging to Ralph, the lead singer in Marcus's band, began to sing: "He doesn't pretend, he's just my best friend, wherever I ride, my dog's by my side. . . ."

Draper stopped and sniffed the air and then began trotting toward the camera, his tongue lolling out of the side of his mouth, looking as if he were smiling. The music faded out, and the video cut to Zoey sitting at her sewing table, talking about how Draper was her inspiration for starting Doggie Duds. And then the music faded back in, quieter now, while Draper and Zoey were walking down the sidewalk. When Ralph stopped singing, you could hear other the other dog owner telling Zoey "Nice outfit" and "Love your dog's outfit. Where did you get it?" and finally "You should start a business!"

At the end, the name Doggie Duds popped up on the screen, along with the URLs for the Sew Zoey blog and the Myfundmaker page.

"That's amazing," Zoey said, taking off the headphones. "How did you . . . When did you do the song?"

"I had written the lyrics before"—Marcus swallowed—"Draper . . . you know. Dan wrote the music and recorded it with Ralph while I was working on editing the video. I just finished up laying the sound track into the video while you were getting your stuff at A Stitch in Time."

"It must have taken you an eternity," Zoey said. "You're the best brother EVER!"

"Can I have that in writing?" Marcus asked.

"As soon as I find my invisible ink pen," Zoey quipped.

She pushed play again. She couldn't hear the sound because the headphones were plugged in, but she could watch Draper, as if he'd come to life again. "We have to send this to Aunt Lulu!" Zoey exclaimed. "She'll love it."

"Let's upload it to the project page first so we

don't forget," Marcus said. "Then we can just send her the video file."

Zoey agreed, and she waited impatiently while the video uploaded, which seemed to take forever.

Marcus dashed off a quick e-mail with the video and a note to Aunt Lulu before heading home.

Two minutes after Zoey and Marcus walked in the front door, the phone rang. It was Aunt Lulu. Marcus put her on speakerphone, so Zoey could hear too.

"Oh, you guys, I just got off of a conference call, and opening that e-mail and finding that video was such a wonderful surprise," Aunt Lulu said. "I'm smiling and crying at the same time. Seeing Draper again, just being so . . . Draper! That look on his face when he was sniffing the air like he'd caught wind of a treat . . ."

"That's because he had," Zoey said. "It was the only way we could get him to frolic."

"Or what passes for frolicking when you're a fourteen-year-old dog," Marcus said.

"Well, I love that you captured Draper being himself. I'll treasure this, always," Aunt Lulu said.

She sounded like she was starting to cry again. "You kids are the best."

As soon as they hung up, Zoey took her bags of fabric and went up to her room. Aunt Lulu definitely needed something to cheer her up, and it was time to get working on her ballroom dance skirt. Having the soft silk chiffon swirling around her ankles while she danced wouldn't make up for missing Draper, but it might make her feel a little better. Zoey laid the material on the table carefully, took out her scissors, and got to work.

CHAPTER 7

Belle of the Ballroom Dance!

You know if you're really miserable, sometimes getting to work on a project, doing something you love for someone you love, makes you feel better. At least it's helped do that for me, kind of. I'm making this for a special someone who might also be feeling a little down right now. She takes ballroom dancing lessons, so I thought I'd make her a skirt that will float when she twirls and swish around her ankles, like on one of those ballroom-dance reality shows.

It's weird, though, to be sewing without Draper resting his head on my foot or thumping his tail when he hears the sound of Marcus or Dad walking down the hallway. If I miss Draper this much, I can't imagine how my aunt feels. She loved the video Marcus made for my Doggie Duds Myfundmaker page (which I hope to be launching very, very soon—stay tuned!). I can't wait for you all to see it!

TTFN,

Zoey

"How was your dentist appointment?" Zoey asked Kate when she sat next to her on the bus the next morning. "Any cavities?"

"What dentist appointment?" Kate said, her face a blank.

"The one you had yesterday after school," Zoey prompted, "so you weren't on the bus going home?"

"Oh! That one!" Kate said. "Uh . . . yeah, good. No cavities. I got a sticker."

But she shifted uncomfortably in her seat. Kate was a really bad liar, and Zoey could see she wasn't telling the truth. It made her wonder what Kate had really been doing yesterday afternoon. Had she and Priti done something without her, just the way the three of them had a sleepover without Libby?

"That's good," Zoey said, but she spent the rest of the ride to school drawing in her sketchbook instead of talking with her friend.

When Zoey got to her locker, she found it adorned with a really cute picture of Draper surrounded by a pretty fabric heart, decorated with sequins and decorative buttons. It was attached to her locker door with a set of dog-shape magnets. One of them even looked a little like Draper. Underneath the picture heart was a note on pink paper:

We miss you, Draper, our doggie friend! Feel better, Zoey! Hugs, Priti and Kate xoxo

That's when Zoey realized what Kate must have been doing after school yesterday and why she'd seemed so evasive about going to the dentist. She'd been trying to keep this a surprise.

The knowledge that her friends weren't excluding her and the sight of Draper's beloved face when she wasn't expecting to see it combined to hit Zoey with a powerful wave of emotion. She grabbed the picture of Draper off her locker and ran to the nearest bathroom, making it past the door just as her tears overflowed.

To her dismay, who should be in the bathroom but Shannon Chang and Bree Sharpe, Ivy's sidekicks. The last thing she wanted was for them to see her crying, especially since they'd joined Ivy in writing mean comments on her blog under different screen names during Spirit Week. She tried to run into a bathroom stall, but Shannon stopped her.

"Are you okay, Zoey?" Shannon asked. "What's the matter?"

She looked genuinely concerned, like the friend Zoey remembered from back in elementary school.

So Zoey told her the truth and didn't hide the tears that were tumbling down her cheeks.

"My aunt's d-dog . . . He d-died this w-weekend," she said with a sniff.

"Oh no! Not Draper!" Shannon exclaimed.

Zoey nodded sadly, surprised Shannon remembered Draper's name. She showed Shannon and Bree the picture.

"What a . . . what a cute dog," Bree said tentatively, looking to Shannon for approval. Shannon smiled, and Bree continued, "Our dog, Bailey, died last year. It was so hard. I still get so sad every time I think about him."

"Really?" Zoey asked, almost waiting for the punch line. But Bree seemed sincere too.

"Yeah, but we got a new dog, Cocoa. See?"

Bree took out her phone and showed Zoey a picture of a small, brown, curly-haired dog on her screen saver.

"Cocoa's so sweet," Shannon said. "Is your aunt going to get another dog? I bet it would make you both feel better."

"I don't know," Zoey said. "I hope so!"

"Hang in there," Bree said as she and Shannon left the bathroom.

"Thanks," Zoey said.

As Zoey washed the tears from her face, she thought about how losing Draper had brought back the sweet Shannon she remembered and had given her something in common with Bree. Maybe it was true what they said about every cloud having a silver lining—even if it was a very big, sad cloud.

Zoey was glad to see Priti and Kate in the hallway before they got to the cafeteria for lunch. She rushed up to them and gave each of them a huge hug.

"Thanks for decorating my locker, you guys. It was *soooo* thoughtful, even if I did end up crying in the bathroom!" she said.

"Oh no!" Kate exclaimed.

"It was supposed to cheer you up, not make you cry," Priti said.

"It's okay. It was really sweet of you to do it," Zoey said. "And believe it or not, Shannon and Bree were in the bathroom, and they were really

nice when they saw me crying. Shannon remembered Draper, and Bree lost her dog last year, so she
knows how I feel."

"No way! Wow," Priti said. "Who'd have thunk?"

Zoey linked her arms through her friends' arms
as they walked down the hall.

"I'm so lucky to have you as my best friends,"
she said. "And . . . that's why I have to ask you guys
about something important before we go to lunch."

"What's that?" Kate asked.

"Would you mind if we . . . made another BFF
bracelet for Libby?" Zoey asked. "I felt so bad yesterday at lunch when we all had them and she didn't."

"I know!" Kate exclaimed. "I felt terrible that I
didn't think to make a bracelet for her. I guess I was
so used to it being you, Priti, and me before Libby
got here. I hope she doesn't think it's because we
don't like her or something."

"So you don't mind her being one of the BFFs,
officially?" Zoey asked. "It's okay for us to be four
peas in a pod instead of three?"

"Of course," Priti said. "Libby's great. And the
more BFFs the merrier!"

Zoey was relieved her friends felt the same way she did about Libby and that they could all be BFFs together.

"Why don't you guys give me your bracelets?" Kate offered. "I'll take them home tonight and remake them with an extra color for Libby and then make a bracelet for Libby, too."

"That's a lot of work," Priti said.

"I don't mind," Kate said. "I feel so bad Libby felt left out. What color bead do you think would be good?"

"Remember those shiny copper-colored ones?" Zoey said. "Those would go well with ours, and they look like Libby's hair."

"Perfect!" Kate said. "I'll start working on the new ones tonight."

That evening, Aunt Lulu came over for dinner, bringing takeout from Zoey and Marcus's favorite Chinese restaurant.

"Fortune cookie time!" Aunt Lulu said, handing each of them a wrapped cookie when they'd finished their main course.

Marcus opened his first.

"'A ship in the harbor is safe, but that's not what ships are built for,'" he read. "I guess I'd better start taking the yacht I don't have out for a sail more often."

"My turn," Mr. Webber said. "'A pleasant surprise is in store for you.' I guess that means you kids are doing the dishes so I can put my feet up and relax."

"Sorry, Dad," Marcus said. "I have to go study so I can get a good job and earn enough money to buy my yacht."

Zoey opened her fortune cookie. "'A good time to start something new.' Oooh! Maybe that means Doggie Duds will be a success!"

"That reminds me—we need to look at the numbers for your project after dinner, don't we?" Lulu asked.

"That would be awesome," Zoey said. "The project page is pretty much done, except for the prices. I need your help with that."

"Okay. But first let's see what the fortune cookie has in store for me," Lulu said, taking hers out of the wrapper and breaking it in half. She stared at the little rectangular slip of paper. "Oh my."

"What is it?" Marcus asked.

"I think it's an omen," Lulu said. "'A new friend will arrive and brighten your day.'" She looked at Marcus and then Zoey. "Speaking of new friends, I've been meaning to ask you two if you'd be willing to come with me to the shelter this weekend to help me find a new canine companion," she said, her eyes glistening. "It's just too quiet at home without Draper. I need some puppy love."

"YES!" Zoey exclaimed. "I've been hoping you'd get a new dog!"

"Really? No dog could replace Draper," Marcus said. "He was one of a kind."

"I know, honey," Aunt Lulu said. "I'm not trying to replace him. Draper will always have a special place in my heart. We'll fall in love with the new dog in a different way. That's the best thing about love—it's not finite. It expands and grows to be however big you need it to be."

"That's right," Mr. Webber said. "I remember when Melissa was pregnant with Zo, I was scared, because I couldn't imagine loving another baby as much as I loved Marcus." He smiled at Zoey. "But then my little girl came along, and the minute I saw her, I thought my heart was going to explode with all that extra love."

"Okay, I'll come to the shelter. Just stop with all the mushy love talk before I regurgitate my kung pao chicken," Marcus said.

Zoey giggled, because she knew that deep down, her brother, Marcus, was just as mushy as the rest of them, especially when it came to dogs.

Zoey's dad said he'd clean up the dishes—and Marcus offered to help—so that Zoey and Aunt Lulu could work on the business plan. Aunt Lulu made Zoey get all her receipts from A Stitch in Time so she knew exactly what her costs were.

"How long did it take you to make the outfit?" she asked.

"About two hours," Zoey said. "But that's because it was the first one. Also because Draper wasn't very cooperative about being fitted. He kept wanting to lie down when I needed him to stand up."

"That was my Draper," Aunt Lulu said with a sad smile.

"So maybe making other ones would take a little less time, because I know how to do it already," Zoey said.

"Let's be conservative and factor in two hours of your time," Lulu said.

She put all the numbers into a spreadsheet and worked out how much Zoey had to charge for each dog outfit to break even.

"But you don't want to just break even—you want to make a profit," Aunt Lulu said.

"Definitely," Zoey said. "Because the whole point of Doggie Duds is to make money for new fabric."

Aunt Lulu looked up prices of dog outfits online.

"We have to get an idea of the market," she said. "See, this outfit is cheaper, but yours is cuter and looks more upscale, so you should be able to get away with charging more."

When they agreed on the price, Zoey talked through the different reward levels with her dad and her aunt.

"Don't forget that you have to work in the costs of the rewards," her aunt said. "And the postage."

"Wow." Zoey sighed. "I never realized how complicated it was to start a business."

"It'll be worth it when the orders start rolling in," Lulu said.

"*If* they start rolling in," Zoey said.

"Well, you can count me in as a customer," Lulu said. "As long as you come help me pick out a dog to wear your wonderful Doggie Duds."

"Deal," Zoey said. "*Oooh*, wait! I almost forgot! I've got a surprise for you."

She ran up to her room and got the ballroom dance skirt she'd made, which she'd wrapped in tissue paper and tied with a piece of colored ribbon. Returning to the kitchen, she handed it to her aunt.

"What's this?" Aunt Lulu asked. "Did I forget it's my birthday?"

"No . . . ," Zoey said. "It's just a special something I made to cheer you up."

Aunt Lulu opened the package.

"Oh, Zoey!" she exclaimed, holding the skirt up to her waist and twirling around. "It's beautiful!"

She hugged Zoey tight. "You're as thoughtful as you are talented. I'm one lucky aunt!"

Aunt Lulu picked Marcus and Zoey up after breakfast that Sunday, and together they drove to the Mapleton Animal Shelter.

"I'm so nervous," Aunt Lulu said. "I feel like I'm going on a first date."

"Did you know *Dad* went on a first date while you were away?" Zoey asked.

"He did? How did it go?" Lulu asked.

"He said she was pretty and nice, and she even laughed at his corny jokes, but there wasn't the same kind of connection he felt on his first date with Mom," Zoey said.

"Well, your mom was an amazing lady. I remember when she told me about that date," Aunt Lulu said. "She said she'd met someone special. And she was right."

"Let's hope you meet your special dog," Marcus said.

"Let's hope!" Lulu agreed.

There were so many cute dogs at the shelter, Zoey wondered how Aunt Lulu would know which one was her special dog. Zoey wanted to take them all home, but she was pretty sure her dad would have something to say about that . . . something like "Take them back, right now!"

Zoey loved a little puggle named Mikey, and Marcus was lobbying for a golden retriever mix called Buddy. But Aunt Lulu wanted to keep looking. And then she said, "Look. There." And she walked over to a crate holding a golden-haired, floppy-mopped poodle mix named Maxi.

"Hello, gorgeous," Lulu crooned, petting the dog through the bars of the crate.

Maxi wagged her tail and licked Aunt Lulu's hand.

"I think I've found my special dog," Aunt Lulu said.

"She's so cute!" Zoey exclaimed.

"Look at those big brown eyes," Marcus said. "They're saying 'Take me home, Aunt Lulu!'"

Aunt Lulu waved to the shelter worker, who came over and asked if they had questions.

"Can you tell us about this darling dog?" asked Aunt Lulu.

"Oh, Maxi's a doll," the shelter worker said. "She's really sweet and playful. She came to us from a family that didn't realize their child was allergic to dogs. They had to bring her here and get a hypo-allergenic breed. The poor kid was heartbroken when they left her, but I promised we'd find her a great home."

"I think you might have just done that," Lulu said. "I just lost my fourteen-year-old dog, Draper, and I've fallen in love with this one."

"Me too," Marcus said.

"Me three," said Zoey.

"Well, you're in luck," the shelter worker said. "She's housebroken and has had all her shots. You can take her home today!"

"Oh . . . I was hoping I could pick her up in a few days," Lulu said. "I've got an on-site decorating consultation this week, and I'd rather not leave her alone the first few days at home after being adopted. I thought it would take a few days to do the paperwork."

"No, unfortunately, we can't hold her for you," the shelter worker said. "Too many people say they'll come back for dogs, and then they don't."

Aunt Lulu gazed at the dog longingly.

"Let me get her out of the crate for you," the shelter worker said.

She got a leash, opened the crate door, and hooked it to the collar on the dog's neck. As soon as the dog was out of the crate, she made a beeline for Aunt Lulu.

"It looks like she's chosen you too, Aunt Lulu," Marcus said.

Aunt Lulu stroked the dog's head. "I think we've chosen each other," she said. "But I don't know what to do. What if someone adopts her before I can come get her?"

Zoey and Marcus exchanged glances.

"What if we took her home?" Zoey suggested. "I mean, if Dad says it's okay."

"Then you can pick her up when your consultation is over," Marcus said. "That way, we'll know she's ours. I mean, yours."

"*Ours*," Aunt Lulu said. "That's a great idea.

Let's call your dad and see what he thinks."

A quick call to Mr. Webber sealed the deal. Aunt Lulu signed all the papers, and the shelter worker handed her Maxi's leash.

"One question," Lulu said. "I'm not crazy about the name Maxi. I don't think it suits her. Can we change it, or will she have some kind of doggie identity crisis?"

"Absolutely, you can change it. We actually recommend our dogs start their new lives with a positive new name to go with it," the shelter worker said. "One tip: Dogs respond well to names with a lot of hard consonants."

"Well, we have a new game to play on the ride home," Lulu said. "Name That Dog!"

The Dog Who Needed a New Name trotted out to the car beside Lulu and jumped into the backseat as soon as Zoey opened the door.

On the ride back to the Webber house, they brainstormed potential names.

"Rosie?" Zoey said.

The dog ignored her.

"She's coffee colored," Marcus observed. "How about Latte or Cappuccino? Cappuccino has a *lot* of hard consonants."

The dog drooled on the window, ignoring him, too.

"Hmm. I don't think she likes it," Zoey said.

"Besides, can you imagine calling for her in the park?" Lulu said, laughing. "I'd sound like I was begging someone to buy me coffee! And a pricey one, at that."

Many other names were tried and rejected before Lulu pulled into the Webber driveway. The trio rattled off the names of their favorite characters from books and movies and looked at street signs for inspiration.

"I think you're going to have to keep working on it while I'm doing the design consultation," Lulu said. "Hopefully, Miss Doggie will let you know when you've come up with a name she likes."

"She's so smart," Zoey said, stroking the dog's ears. "I'm sure she will."

----------- CHAPTER 8 ----------

Cute as a Button!

We have a new dog! Well, when I say "we," I mean Aunt Lulu, but the Dog Formerly Known as Maxi (and currently known as Doggie No Name; Jane *Doggie*, and Here, Girl since we're still on the hunt for the perfect name) is staying with us for a few days.

But we're having a real problem finding the right name. Yesterday, when we got home with her, we sat around the kitchen table, trying out different ones. Doggie just raised an eyebrow and ignored us, finally curling up into a ball of fur under the table and settling down for a nap.

Even though she doesn't have her forever name yet, she has already found a forever place in our hearts. She is sooooooooo cute! She's here with me now, sitting under my worktable, just like Draper used to, looking up at me with her big brown eyes and her button nose. . . . I just bought a bunch of buttons and none of them are as cute as this dog. Wait a minute. Buttons! That's it! She's cute as a button . . . so that should be her new name! I just tried calling her Buttons, and she got up and wagged her tail and came and licked my hand. I think Doggie No Name just chose Buttons! I hope Aunt Lulu agrees.

And here's some more good news! I'm almost ready to launch the Doggie Duds campaign! Aunt Lulu helped me work out all the business stuff, and I'm putting the final touches on the launch page. Stay tuned! I can't wait for you all to see what I've got planned!

"I'm here!" Aunt Lulu said as she came in through the front door. "Where's my puppy?"

She'd promised to visit every night until she could take the dog home.

At the sound of Aunt Lulu's voice, the dog got up from where she was sitting nestled next to Zoey's feet, and went running toward the front door.

Zoey heard Aunt Lulu fussing and crooning over the puppy, telling her she'd brought her presents. The pooch was not going to lack for anything, especially love, that was for sure!

"Aunt Lulu, she's chosen her name!" Zoey exclaimed.

"What's that?" Aunt Lulu asked.

Zoey walked to the opposite end of the hall.

"Buttons! Come here, Buttons!" she called.

Buttons pricked up her ears at the sound of her name and scampered straight to Zoey.

"Good girl, Buttons!" Zoey said. "Buttons, sit!"

And the dog sat at Zoey's feet, looking up at her expectantly with her big brown eyes.

"Look at that! She has chosen her name, hasn't

she?" Aunt Lulu chuckled. "How did you come up with Buttons?"

"I was looking at the cool buttons I'd bought at A Stitch in Time for my Doggie Duds outfits and thinking how she is cute as a button with her little button nose and . . . well, I tried the name, and she liked it," Zoey explained.

"Well, Buttons it is!" Lulu said. "I'll get her tags engraved tomorrow."

Aunt Lulu fed the brand-new Buttons her dinner and cooked for the family as a thank-you for looking after her dog.

"So when is the big launch of your Doggie Duds business?" she asked Zoey when they'd finished dinner.

"I wasn't sure what to do about the rewards and the video," Zoey said. "Like the basic reward is a sketch of Draper's paw print—but I can't do that now, can I?"

"What about a paw print from Buttons?" her father suggested. "I don't think people would mind, if you explain what happened."

"I guess," Zoey said. "But what about the video?

I don't want to change it because Draper was the inspiration behind the whole thing—"

"Not to mention it took me *forever* to make that video," Marcus said.

"Well, yeah, that, too," Zoey agreed. "And you did an amazing job."

"Leave it," Aunt Lulu said. "You can always add additional photos and videos to your page, right?"

"Yes," Zoey said. And that's when she looked at Buttons and got an idea.

"Can I be excused?" she asked. "I have . . . something important I have to do."

"Okay," her father said. "Just put your dishes in the dishwasher first."

"See you tomorrow, honey," Aunt Lulu said.

Zoey cleaned her place, kissed her aunt good night, and then raced up to her room. She picked one of the fabrics she'd gotten on sale in the remnant bin at A Stitch in Time and chose some buttons to match. But one critical thing was missing.

"Buttons!" she called. "Come here, girl!"

She heard the padding of paws up the stairs, and Buttons came trotting down the hall to her room.

"Good girl," Zoey said. "Now let me measure you. If you're going to be the new spokesdog for Doggie Duds, you need a seriously cute outfit!"

Buttons stood patiently, wagging her tail, while Zoey measured her.

"You're a lot more cooperative than Draper was," Zoey told her. "You could be on *Fashion Show*dog.

Buttons licked Zoey's nose.

"Okay, I'm done," Zoey said.

Buttons sniffed around the room. She seemed particularly interested in the chic-on-the-cheap dress Zoey had made, which was on the floor, waiting to be washed so Zoey could wear it to be twins with Libby.

I really need to do that, Zoey thought.

"No, Buttons. Leave my dress alone," Zoey said. She picked it up off the floor and put it on the back of her chair.

Buttons looked up at Zoey, then settled under the sewing table, just like Draper had done.

Zoey adjusted the pattern she'd made for Draper's outfit for Buttons's measurements and started cutting the fabric. She decided to cut some extra fabric to make ruffles. Buttons's outfit needed some girly flair. If it turned out well, maybe she could offer Doggie Duds customers two choices of outfits—the original Draper and the more feminine Buttons.

But first she had to make Buttons's outfit. She picked a spool of thread that matched the fabric, threaded it into the sewing machine, and then got to work, edging fabric and making buttonholes.

It took her almost as long as it did to make the original Draper outfit, because of the ruffles, but it was worth the effort. When she tried it on Buttons, it fit perfectly.

Zoey took Buttons down to the living room, where Marcus and Dad were watching TV, to model the latest Doggie Duds creation.

"What do you think?" she asked.

"Cute," her dad said.

"Buttons seems to like it," Marcus observed, watching the dog prance around the room, tail wagging.

"Can you take a picture of her in it?" Zoey asked. "I want to add it to the Doggie Duds page."

"Sure," Mr. Webber said.

He went to get his digital camera, the one that took really good quality pictures.

Marcus and Zoey acted as dog wranglers, with Zoey standing next to Buttons, just out of camera range, encouraging her to sit, and Marcus standing behind Mr. Webber with a toy, squeaking it to get Buttons's attention, just before their dad took the picture.

"I've got to admit, that is one incredibly cute dog," Mr. Webber said as he reviewed the pictures.

"And the outfit is pretty adorable too, don't you think?" Zoey asked.

"The outfit makes the dog even cuter, definitely," he said, ruffling Zoey's hair. He took the memory card out of the camera and handed it to her. "Okay, kiddo. Go get this business launched."

Zoey picked the photo that showed off both Buttons and the ruffled outfit to the best advantage and uploaded it to her project page. Before she made her campaign live, though, she decided she needed to update the description to let pledgers know about Draper.

Since we created the video for this project,
Draper, the star of the video and the
inspiration for Doggie Duds, has sadly left
us for dog heaven. ☹ He'll always be with
us in our hearts. I'd like you to meet our new
Doggie Duds spokespuppy, Buttons, who I'm
sure you'll all agree is as cute as a button
in her Doggie Duds outfit, complete with a
girly ruffle. Supporters of Doggie Duds who
contribute at the dog outfit level can choose
if they want the Draper or the Buttons. I'll
also be basing the paw print drawings off
Buttons's paws, not Draper's.

    Thank you for considering the Doggie
Duds project!

Zoey read through the campaign page over and
over, checking for mistakes. Then she took her laptop downstairs and got her father to check it before
they launched it.

"Looks good to me, honey," her dad said. "You
can go ahead and make it official. Good luck!"

"Yeah. Make lots of money!" Marcus said.

Her finger trembling with nervousness and

excitement, Zoey pushed publish, and with that, the project went live. Doggie Duds was in business . . . assuming people pledged.

She texted her friends and her aunt Lulu to tell them and asked them to tell everyone they knew. Lulu texted back to say she'd already made a pledge, and she would send an e-mail blast to her friends. Libby texted back to say that her mom was online right now ordering the Draper for Chester. Zoey checked the website, and sure enough, the campaign was already at 4 percent of its goal of five hundred dollars. The goal had sounded too high to Zoey at first. It was almost the amount Aunt Lulu had come up with to cover materials for outfits and rewards, with some money left over for Zoey's fabric fund. Not bad for the first twenty minutes! Zoey announced each new pledge to her dad and Marcus as they came in.

"I don't want you up all night checking how much money is coming in," her dad warned. "Sleep and school have to come first."

"I know." Zoey sighed, but she couldn't help

sneaking another glimpse at the web page to see if any more pledges had come in.

It was hard enough to sit through social studies with Mr. Dunn at the best of times, but when she was desperate to know how her Doggie Duds campaign was going, Zoey found it even harder to concentrate. She could just sneak out her smartphone and check the Myfundmaker website under her desk without him seeing, right?

Step one: She *accidentally* dropped her pencil next to her backpack, which was on the floor next to her desk.

Step two: When she leaned down to pick up her pencil, she just happened to slip her hand into the pocket on the side of her backpack and palm her phone.

Step three: She dropped the phone into her lap, all the while keeping her eyes fixed on Mr. Dunn, as if social studies was the only thing on her mind.

Step four: As soon as Mr. Dunn turned to the whiteboard, she searched for the Myfundmaker website. *Come on, hurry up,* she thought. The

Internet at school was really slow compared to home.

Mr. Dunn turned back to the class. Zoey dropped the phone back into her lap. The site had finally loaded, but she'd forgotten she had to log in. *Okay, Mr. Dunn, turn back to the whiteboard,* she thought.

But Mr. Dunn was in one of his calling-on-students-at-random moods. "Mr. Monaco, what was 'the shot heard round the world'?"

Zoey's friend Gabe, who'd been doodling in his notebook in the seat by her, started.

"Oh! Um . . . the first shot fired at Lexington?"

"Correct," Mr. Dunn said. "So you *are* paying attention, good."

He turned back to the whiteboard, and Zoey half listened while she entered her username and password into the Myfundmaker website and waited impatiently for her page to come up. *Come on, come on . . .*

Wow! Doggie Duds was already 25 percent funded! Zoey couldn't believe—

"Miss Webber, I'm getting the impression I don't

have your full attention," Mr. Dunn said, walking toward her desk.

Uh-oh. Not good.

"Are you being distracted by an electronic device that is forbidden during class, by any chance?" asked Mr. Dunn, standing right over Zoey.

There was no way she could put her phone away without him seeing. The only thing she could do was be honest.

"Yes, Mr. Dunn," she confessed, handing him her phone.

"You'll get this back at the end of class," he said. He glanced at the screen. "Doggie Duds?" he muttered under his breath, shaking his head as he walked back to the front of the classroom.

Now Zoey had to worry about her punishment. Would Mr. Dunn give her detention or send her to see Ms. Austen? She really didn't want to disappoint her favorite principal . . . or her dad. Worrying made the rest of class drag on even longer.

But when she went up to Mr. Dunn's desk to get her phone back, he asked, "What's so important about this Doggie Duds website that it made you break school rules to look at it during class?"

"It's my new Myfundmaker project," Zoey explained. "I just launched it last night, so . . . well, I guess I'm really excited to see how it's going. I'm sorry about looking at my phone in class."

"What made you pick Doggie Duds as a project?" Mr. Dunn asked.

Zoey explained about her need to raise money for more fabric and how Draper's outfit and all the compliments it received inspired her to create Doggie Duds. And she told him how Draper passed away before she could launch the project, but now Buttons was the new spokesdog.

Mr. Dunn handed her the phone. "Miss Webber, I'm a big believer in free market and in encouraging young people to be entrepreneurs, so I'm going to let you off this time. But don't let it happen again."

"It won't!" Zoey promised, relieved. "Thank you, Mr. Dunn!"

When she met her friends at lunch, Zoey told them about her miraculous escape from Dunntention and updated them on how her project was going.

"That's amazing!" Kate said. "I knew it would be a success!"

"Not quite yet," Zoey said. "But it's a good start. And I still haven't posted the link on my blog yet. I'm doing that tonight."

"Are most of them big pledges who know you?" Libby asked.

Zoey logged into the site again to check.

"A few of them are—like Aunt Lulu and your mom," she said. "But most of them are small pledges. Lots of small ones add up quickly!"

"You're going to be busy drawing paw prints," Priti said.

"I know," Zoey said. "Oh! That reminds me. Do you want to come over after school today and meet Buttons? Then maybe, if you don't mind, you could help me start making the rewards for the first-level pledges. It's going to take a while to cut all the cards and address envelopes and draw clothes and paw prints."

"Sure!" Kate said. "I don't have any practices today. And I can't wait to meet Buttons!"

"As long as Mom says yes, count me in," Priti said.

"I can't," Libby said, sighing. "I've got a doctor's appointment. Believe me, I'd *much* rather meet Buttons!"

Zoey still hadn't gotten around to washing her chic-on-the-cheap dress, but she'd only worn it that one time to the mall. She figured maybe she could get away without washing it, just this once.

"How about we wear our twins dresses tomorrow?" Zoey asked. "We've been meaning to do that for a while. And we'll make a date for you to meet Buttons soon."

"Sounds like a plan," Libby said, smiling. "Twinsies tomorrow!"

When Kate and Priti walked in with Zoey after school, Buttons could barely contain her excitement. She spun around in circles, her tail wagging furiously. Then, when Kate bent down to pet her, she ran away and fetched a toy and came back with it in her mouth, squeaking noisily, obviously wanting to play with her new friends.

"She is *sooo* cute," Priti said. "I wonder if Mom would let us get a dog."

"I thought she had a strict no-pet policy?" Zoey asked.

"She does," Priti admitted. "But look at this face! Doesn't it make you melt?"

"It does, but owning a dog is a lot of work. It's easier just to visit one," Kate said. "Right, Buttons?"

Buttons wagged her tail and dropped the toy at Zoey's feet for her to throw. Zoey tossed the toy, and Buttons chased it and came back squeaking as soon as she fetched it.

After a snack, the girls got to work on the pledge rewards. They decided to work downstairs on the dining room table, because they had more room to spread out and create an assembly line. Zoey printed out a list of the names and addresses of all the people who'd pledged at the paw-print level. Since Kate had the neatest handwriting, she was assigned to addressing envelopes, and Priti was chief cutter, responsible for cutting the big sheets of white cardstock into small paw-print-sized squares. Zoey took Buttons out into the yard and pressed her paw into the dirt in the flower bed. Then she pressed it onto one of the small card squares to get an imprint to copy for her drawings.

"Thanks, Buttons," she said. Buttons licked her face.

As soon as Buttons came back inside, she sat down and started licking her dirty paw.

"Someone doesn't like having dirty feet!" Kate said.

"Maybe my mom would like a dog like Buttons after all." Priti laughed.

"What's not to like?" Zoey asked.

Zoey started sketching copies of Buttons's paw print while her friends worked on their tasks.

"Have you met the new guy at school yet?" Priti asked.

"What new guy?" Zoey wondered.

"You mean that guy Dean?" Kate said. "He's in my math class."

"He transferred to Mapleton Prep this week," Priti said. "He's sooooooo cute."

"How did I not notice him if he's so cute?" Zoey asked.

"Because you've been so wrapped up in Doggie Duds," Kate said.

"That's true," Zoey said. "I have been kind of obsessed with getting it launched, and now that it is, I want to check every five minutes to see if more pledges have come in."

"Well, you can't let yourself get so obsessed that you don't even notice a guy as cute as Dean Sharma," Priti said. "That's just . . . not healthy!"

"I'll make sure to keep my eyes wide open," Zoey promised.

"But don't forget, I saw him first!" Priti warned.

"I won't!" Zoey said. "Besides, I'm going to be too busy making dog outfits to have time for much else."

Buttons came tearing around the table with something in her mouth.

"What's she got?" Zoey exclaimed.

"I don't know, but I hope she doesn't swallow it," Kate said.

"No, Buttons! Leave it!" Zoey ordered.

Buttons turned and bolted into the kitchen. Zoey, Kate, and Priti gave chase.

Buttons seemed to think this was a great game and scampered into the living room, tail wagging.

"Spread out and surround her!" Priti ordered.

The girls managed to corner the playful puppy between the coffee table and the sofa, and retrieved what turned out to be a scrap of fabric from Zoey's bedroom from her mouth.

"Puppies are really cute, but they're also a lot of work," Zoey said.

"But supercute," said Priti, stroking Buttons.

By the time her friends left, there was a neat stack of envelopes, addressed and ready to be mailed with paw-print rewards inside for the first round of pledges. Zoey made sure to keep a careful check of whom she'd sent them to, so no one was left out. She breathed a sigh of relief. Paw-print rewards were done! And Buttons was curled up quietly, sleeping. At least for now . . .

------------ CHAPTER 9 ------------

Signed, Sealed, and (Almost) Delivered

Doggie Duds is officially launched! Check out the project page and share it with your friends! It's already 25 percent funded, which is really amazing. I thought it would be all big pledges from my family, but it's not. There are lots of small pledges from people I don't know, which is exciting, and it's amazing how it adds up!

Thanks to Priti and Kate (many hands make light work!), everyone who has pledged so far will be getting their paw-print drawings really soon. They are signed, sealed, and waiting to be delivered. My hand hurts from drawing so many! But I'm not complaining—not at all. I'm *so* grateful to everyone who pledged to the project. A special thank-you to CrossStitchGal, who said she'd be getting an outfit for her family's Norfolk terrier, Cookie. I saw the pictures of him on your blog, and he's such a cutie pie! He'll look adorable in his Draper outfit.

Thanks to my "many hands," I've got some extra squares of cardstock cut for future pledges that come, because the campaign still runs for another week. So there's still plenty of time to get your drawing of Buttons's paw print if you pledge (hint! hint!). Meanwhile, I'm looking forward to wearing my chic-on-the-cheap dress tomorrow—Libby and I are going to repeat our twin act at school. I bet that will turn a few heads. . . .

When Zoey went to get dressed the next morning, there was a slight problem. Actually, a major problem. She couldn't find her chic-on-the-cheap dress anywhere.

It's got to be here somewhere, she thought. *I could have sworn I put it out on the back of my chair the other day.*

"Buttons, have you seen my dress?" she asked the puppy, who was sitting waiting for her by the side of her bed.

Zoey looked in her closet again, because she really didn't want to disappoint Libby. Finally, after she checked under her chair again, she looked under her worktable. There it was, on the floor, wrinkled and . . . wet?

When Zoey pulled it out, she realized that it wasn't wet with water, either.

"*Ewwww!*" she shouted, then looked at Buttons, who was giving her puppy dog eyes. "Buttons! Bad dog!"

Now what am I going to do? Zoey thought.

"What happened?" her father asked, sticking his head in the doorway.

"Buttons peed on my dress!" Zoey exclaimed. "The one Libby is expecting me to wear today so we can be twins."

"I guess Buttons isn't quite as 'fully house-broken' as advertised," he said.

Buttons slunk out of the door and hid behind Mr. Webber's knees, her tail between her legs.

"She knows she did something bad," Zoey said. "Look at her."

"It could be she's a little unsettled by the new environment," her dad said, rubbing Buttons between her ears. "We should cut her a little slack, don't you think?"

"I guess," Zoey agreed grumpily. "But what do I tell Libby? The dog peed on my outfit? It sounds even lamer than 'the dog ate my homework'!"

"You'd better find something else to wear or you're going to miss the bus," he said.

Her father shut the door, and Zoey grabbed a pair of jeans and the nearest shirt she could find. She slipped into her Converse, grabbed her back-pack and a granola bar, and raced to the bus stop. She made it there just as the bus was pulling up.

"Hey, I thought you were wearing the twin dress with Libby today," Kate said, when Zoey sat next to her on the bus.

"I was," said Zoey. "But Buttons *rained on my parade*, if you catch my drift."

Kate tried not to giggle. "She *didn't!*"

"Oh yes, she did!"

"Oh, Zoey . . ." Kate was really trying to look sympathetic, but it was hard when she couldn't stop giggling. "I'm sorry, it's just . . ."

Zoey started laughing too. "I know. I can laugh about it now. But I'm worried Libby's going to be upset."

"She'll understand. I mean, you couldn't exactly wear it with Eau de Wee Wee on it, could you?" Kate said.

"Yuck! No!" Zoey exclaimed. "No one would want to come anywhere near me!"

Zoey hoped to find Libby before school, so she could explain her dress disaster. She waited for Libby's bus to arrive, but Libby wasn't on it. She tried going to Libby's locker and she wasn't there. Zoey realized if she didn't hurry, she was going to be late for first period—Mr. Dunn. He'd let her off the hook yesterday, and she didn't want to push her luck. She arrived to his classroom breathless, just as the bell rang.

Zoey still hadn't seen Libby when it was time for art, their first class together. Zoey peeked into the classroom but didn't see Libby, so she went back to Libby's locker, looking for her. She wanted to explain to Libby what Buttons did, so Libby wouldn't think she'd forgotten about their twin plan. But Libby wasn't at her locker. It was as if she'd disappeared from the face of Mapleton Prep.

Brrrrriiiiiiiiing. Oh no! Zoey was late for art. It was definitely not her day.

"I'm sorry I'm late," Zoey told Mrs. Morris, the art teacher.

"Just give me your pass and take a seat," said Mrs. Morris.

"Um . . . I don't have a pass," Zoey confessed. "I was looking for Libby."

Mrs. Morris looked at Zoey over her glasses as the rest of the class started laughing.

"Libby came to class early. She's right over there," Mrs. Morris said, pointing to the back of the class where Libby was sitting just out of the sight line of where Zoey had glanced into the room earlier, wearing the twin dress and looking stone-faced. "Take a seat and see me after class."

Fortunately, there was an empty seat next to Libby. Zoey slid into it and right away Libby whispered, "Why aren't you wearing the dress? Don't you want to be twins?"

"I do!" Zoey whispered. "It's just that—"

"Zoey, you've already disrupted class by arriving late. Please don't disrupt things even more by talking," Mrs. Morris interrupted.

Zoey blushed. She wasn't a troublemaker, and art was one of her favorite classes. But she could tell Libby was really upset she wasn't wearing the twin dress, and she was desperate to explain to her friend that it wasn't because she didn't want to—it was because she'd experienced complications of a wet and smelly nature.

Surreptitiously tearing a piece of paper from her notebook, Zoey scribbled a quick explanation of the dress disaster and tried to get Libby's attention so she could pass it to her.

"I'm not sure what's gotten in to you today, Zoey Webber, but if I have to speak to you one more time, you're going straight to the principal," Mrs. Morris said. "Are we clear?"

Zoey crumpled the note in her fist and sat up straight, her eyes fixed on Mrs. Morris. "Yes, Mrs. Morris."

As desperate as Zoey was to explain things to Libby, she couldn't risk being sent to Ms. Austen for misbehaving in class. Zoey really looked up to Ms. Austen, and the last thing she wanted to do was to see a disappointed look in Ms. Austen's eyes. Telling Libby why she wasn't wearing the dress would have to wait until after class, even though Zoey could almost feel an invisible wall growing between them, and she wanted to tear it down before it got any higher.

But when class ended, Libby leaped out of her chair and raced out of the classroom before Zoey could say a word. Zoey gathered her books and tried to catch up, but her legs were a lot shorter than her friend's, and Libby was long gone by the time Zoey got to the hallway. Zoey knew she couldn't afford to be late to any more classes, so the explanation was going to have to wait until after gym, when she saw Libby at lunchtime.

She was getting changed after gym, hoping to get to lunch early to catch Libby, when Shannon came up to her. Shannon looked over her shoulder before she spoke, to make sure Ivy wasn't within earshot.

"Hey, Zoey—did your aunt get a new dog yet?" she asked.

"Yeah, she did. Her name's Buttons," Zoey told her. "Do you want to see a picture?"

"Sure!" Shannon said, checking over her shoulder again.

Zoey showed Shannon the screensaver on her phone. It was a picture of Buttons in the Buttons outfit.

"She's so cute! And I love that outfit! Where did you get it?"

"I made it," Zoey said. "I'm doing a Myfundmaker project called Doggie Duds to sell the outfits."

"That's so cool!" Shannon said. "Well . . . good luck, and congrats on the new puppy. I've gotta go."

Zoey finished getting dressed and raced up to the cafeteria, hoping to catch Libby before their friends arrived, so they could talk privately. But all their friends were already sitting at the lunch table, and Libby still looked distinctly unhappy.

"Libby, I'm *so* sorry I'm not wearing the twin dress!" Zoey said. "I've been running around looking for you all day to try to explain. That's why I was late for class."

"So why aren't you wearing it?" Libby asked.

Kate started giggling, which just seemed to make Libby even more upset.

"It was Buttons," Zoey explained. "Even though they said she was fully housebroken at the shelter, she apparently isn't. Or maybe like Dad said, she's unsettled because she's in a new place or something. But anyway . . . I'd put the dress on my chair, all ready to wear, and it must have fallen off the chair and Buttons PEED ON IT!" Zoey said in disgust.

"Oh no!" Libby exclaimed.

"Gross!" Priti said. "Now I'm *glad* Mom doesn't let us have pets."

"I didn't realize she'd done it until this morning when I went to get dressed," Zoey explained. "It was too late to call you—and I almost missed the bus as it was! I'm so sorry."

Libby exhaled before speaking. "I thought maybe you forgot, or . . . maybe you didn't want to be twins with me after all. I'm sorry I got so upset."

"It's okay," Zoey said. "I'll wash it over the weekend, and then we can wear them on Monday."

"Great," Libby said with a big smile on her face. "It's kinda soon to wear it again, but I don't mind."

With everyone feeling happier, the girls settled down to eat lunch.

"Hey, what happened to your bracelets?" Libby asked.

Zoey gave Priti and Kate a meaningful look. They were definitely doing the right thing by making a BFF bracelet for Libby.

"I've got them at home," Kate explained. "I had

to . . . fix them. I realized I'd made a mistake on the pattern."

"Oh, that must be a pain," Libby said.

"No," Kate said. "It's really no trouble at all."

The first thing Zoey did when she got home from school—after greeting Buttons and letting her out for a bathroom break in the yard—was check how her dogwear campaign was going.

When she saw the number of new pledges, Zoey blinked several times to make sure she wasn't having a problem with her eyes. There were more than seventy-five new orders for Doggie Duds— including one from . . . Mr. Dunn! There was also a flood of smaller pledges from fans who said they had seen her on *Fashion Showdown* and started reading her blog. The small pledges were really starting to add up, and the campaign had already reached its goal and was still going strong.

That was the good news.

The bad news was that Zoey had no idea how she was going to keep up with the demand for the rewards promised at each funding level. After homework, she spent the rest of the afternoon doing paw-print drawings. She was still working when Aunt Lulu arrived to see Buttons that evening, bringing takeout for dinner.

"My hand already aches, and I still have more paws to draw!" Zoey groaned as they all sat at the dinner table. "And I have to cut out more cards, because I've used up all the ones Priti and Kate did for me. And that's before I even get to making all the dog outfits and drawing the clothing sketches . . ."

"No one ever said being a successful businesswoman was easy, Zo," her dad said. "Just ask your aunt!"

"True enough. But maybe you could make life a little easier for yourself, Zoey, by making a rubber stamp of Buttons's paw print instead of drawing each one by hand."

"Could I do that?" Zoey asked, nursing her sore hand. "Won't people be upset?"

"I think if you explain what's happened, people will understand," Aunt Lulu said. "It's worth a try."

"Yeah, you won't be able to sew anything if you

get repetitive stress injury from drawing all the rewards," Marcus pointed out.

The risk of injuring her hand and not being able to sew was enough to convince Zoey. After dinner, Marcus helped her search online for a local office supply store that made rubber stamps to order.

"They even do rush jobs," he said. He helped Zoey scan and upload one of the paw-print drawings, and Aunt Lulu let Zoey pay by using her credit card, telling her she could reimburse her when she had some profits from Doggie Duds.

"It says it'll be delivered tomorrow by six p.m.," Marcus said.

"Great!" Zoey said. "So I can cut up the cards and get the envelopes addressed and ready to go, and then tomorrow I can stamp like crazy."

That night, Zoey updated her Myfundmaker page:

> You guys are amazing. The number of
> pledges has been beyond my wildest
> dreams. But that's meant I've had to make
> a slight change to one of the rewards

to prevent what I call "seriously aching
hand" and what my brother, Marcus, calls
"repetitive stress injury." Since I want to
keep drawing and sewing for many decades
to come, I've ordered a special custom
stamp made from the drawing of Buttons's
paw print. I'll be using the stamp instead of
drawing each paw print individually. I hope
you understand!

But it wasn't just the rewards Zoey was most
worried about—it was disappointing everyone.
She'd made all these promises. How was she going
to keep them?

CHAPTER 10

The *Upside-Down* Side of Success

You know how you think that you can never have too much, say . . . chocolate, but then after Halloween, when you and your friends sit around and eat all the best candy you got while trick-or-treating, you feel kind of sick. You're afraid you're never going to be able to eat chocolate again. Well, that's kind of how I'm feeling about my Doggie Duds campaign right now. Don't get me wrong—I'm so excited and grateful that so many people have pledged. It's been amazing! I couldn't believe my eyes yesterday when I came home and looked at the number of orders. It's just . . . I'm feeling a little overwhelmed by success. I'm a teensy bit worried that after overdoing it by sewing all these doggie outfits, I might get sick of sewing for real.

Last night I had a nightmare that I was drowning in orders for Doggie Duds. I was happy when my alarm went off to wake me up this morning and I realized it was only a dream. Except it isn't a dream, because I *am* drowning in orders. I'm not sure how I'm going to keep up with all the rewards and orders for dog outfits without quitting school and becoming a one-girl 24/7 sewing factory. I mean, I love sewing and all—but at this rate I'm going to be sewing Doggie Duds at my high school graduation—and that's before I even think about doing homework for middle school! I'm going to use some of the drawings that didn't make it into my blog posts for the fashion sketch rewards, to save time. But this one is brand-new: I've been feeling like

I've had to juggle a lot lately, which made me think of the circus, which made me come up with this sketch, just for fun.

It's so crazy, because I started this whole campaign because people kept asking me to make dog outfits for them and I was running out of money for fabric. Now I have more than enough money for fabric, but there's no way I have the time to sew all the outfits by myself. Marcus said this situation is like the one in a book he's reading for class—it's called *Catch-22*. No matter how you look at it, there's no perfect solution.

When Zoey came home from school the next day, she couldn't face checking her Myfundmaker page. The thought of having to add even one more dog outfit or reward to her already long to-do list made her want to bury her head in her pillow. Even Buttons scampering around her feet playfully with a squeaky toy couldn't cheer her up. Aunt Lulu was coming to pick her up tonight, because it was the last day of her on-site consultation. Zoey was going to miss Buttons, but it would also be a relief not to worry about her peeing on her clothes or chewing anything she wasn't supposed to.

Zoey decided to check her blog, because her readers always seemed to have good advice. She wasn't disappointed. Fashionsista, her fashion fairy godmother, left a long comment for her:

Instead of sending a gift to you, I'm sending some valuable advice! If you're getting this many orders (which is a good thing, I'd like to remind you!), it might be time to consider scaling up your business and finding a source to manufacture the outfits for you. I recommend using a wonderful website called Manufactory.com, which helps small designers find factories and materials to mass-produce their designs. Get your dad or aunt to help you with the quote pro-cess. It's pretty straightforward.

Sew proud of you,

Fashionsista

A few other readers seconded the suggestion. The thought that she might be able to get someone else to make the dog outfits gave Zoey the courage to check the Doggie Duds page. She hadn't wanted to check it earlier because she was already over-whelmed by the current number of orders. Now that she had a plan for how to fulfill them, she logged in and took another look.

There were thirty-one new orders for dog out-fits, which made her extra glad about Manufactory. There was no way she'd ever be able to make more than one hundred dog outfits by herself! Not to mention there were another eighty-nine small pledges requiring paw-print rewards and eigh-teen needing fashion sketches, and a grand total of five super-duper pledges who would need one of each reward. One of the pledges was from Fashionsista!

It was superexciting, but it was also starting to make her head spin. Thank goodness the paw-print stamp was on the way! At least now she only had to cut up the cards. Maybe she could get Marcus to drive her to the office supply store to buy more cardstock—then she could use the big paper cut-ter instead of using scissors to cut the squares.

Buttons stood on her hind legs and dropped the

squeaky toy in Zoey's lap, her tail wagging and her warm brown eyes sparkling hopefully.

"You want to play?" Zoey asked.

Buttons dropped to all fours, spun around in a circle, and barked.

"You're right, Buttons. All work and no play is going to make me a dull, miserable girl," Zoey said. "Let's go out for walkies."

Buttons hadn't yet learned the word "walkies" like Draper, but she knew Zoey was getting up from her desk and paying attention to her, and that was enough to get her into a state of tail-wagging excitement.

Zoey put on Buttons's outfit and clipped on her leash, and together they went into the afternoon sunshine. Buttons trotted by Zoey's side, stopping at frequent intervals to sniff interesting scents and to leave her "signature." The sky was a vivid blue, the air chill and crisp. Zoey began to feel less anxious about everything she had to do. Tonight she'd ask her dad and aunt Lulu to help her with the Manufactory site. She was still thinking about it when she heard someone calling her name.

It was Mrs. Silverberg, the owner of the cute little Shih Tzu. "Hi, Zoey!" she said. "Remember me? I just ordered the Buttons outfit for Princess. So glad you decided to sell dog clothes!"

"Thanks," Zoey said. "There have been so many orders that I'm actually looking into seeing if I can get them mass-produced . . . but I'll sew yours, I mean Princess's, myself!"

"I knew they'd be popular. They're just adorable," Mrs. Silverberg said. "I was sorry to hear about Draper, though. He was a lovely old dog. Is this Buttons?"

"Yes, it is," Zoey said.

Buttons was busy sniffing the Shih Tzu's rear end.

"Oh my goodness. Stop that, Buttons!" Zoey admonished.

"Honey, she's being a dog," Mrs. Silverberg said, laughing. "That's what they do."

"It's so gross!" Zoey said.

"Not to them, it isn't," she replied, smiling. "They're just saying hello. Well, good luck with the rest of the campaign! Princess is looking forward to being a model for Doggie Duds."

"Great!" Zoey said. "I'll get to work on Princess's outfit right away!"

At dinner, Zoey brought the family up to date on the latest order numbers for Doggie Duds and the fund-raising totals.

"Wow!" Marcus said. "Maybe my band should do a Myfundmaker campaign to record an album."

"Maybe you should," Mr. Webber said. "But there's also supply and demand."

"That's right," Lulu agreed. "Zoey had an interesting product and there weren't a lot of similar projects."

"You mean she found a niche to fill with crazy dog owners?" Marcus said.

"Watch it, buddy. I'm one of those 'crazy' dog owners," Lulu said.

"Princess, the Shih Tzu down the street, can't wait to model her Buttons outfit," Zoey said. "At least that's what her owner, Mrs. Silverberg, told me today. She didn't seem crazy. She seemed really nice."

"Well, what I want to know is: How are you going to make all these outfits and keep up with your schoolwork?" her dad asked.

"That's what I wanted to talk to you about," Zoey said. "Fashionsista—you know, the one from my blog?—she came to the rescue again! She recommended using a website called Manufactory.com to find a factory and materials to mass-produce the outfits instead of me having to make them all myself."

"That's going to cut into your profits," Lulu warned. "But it's probably a good idea so your grades don't suffer."

"Also, so I can have a *life*," Zoey said. "Otherwise, I'd have to sew Doggie Duds every minute I'm not at school or doing homework."

Lulu and Mr. Webber exchanged glances.

"Let's look at this manufacturing site after dinner," Dad said.

With the help of Dad and Aunt Lulu, Zoey got a quote from the website for sourcing the material and making the outfits. Aunt Lulu went through the numbers with Zoey and showed her that she'd still be making a profit, although a smaller one. The orders would start shipping in one month.

"You'll have to let the people who ordered know," Aunt Lulu said, "so they aren't expecting the outfits to arrive next week or that you are making them all yourself."

So Zoey wrote an update on the Doggie Duds Myfundmaker page:

> To everyone who has ordered Doggie Duds:
> First of all—THANK YOU!! This has been success waaaaaay behind my wildest dreams—and that became a problem, because I realized there was no way I could make all the outfits you've ordered by myself. So I took expert advice, and I'm having the outfits manufactured. The bad news is that it's going to take a little longer to get them, and I won't be sewing them personally—but the good news is, Doggie Duds is in business! Thanks again for supporting my project!
> Puppy love,
> Zoey

"Congratulations, Zoey," Aunt Lulu said when she left to go home that evening with Buttons. "You're turning into a real fashion designer with an actual business. You're not just a one-girl show anymore."

The thought made Zoey feel very grown-up. Zoey Webber, fashion designer—for real.

Over the weekend, Zoey was busy making dog outfits for the local pledges to Doggie Duds. She wanted to make sure they got their outfits quickly, since they were the ones who encouraged her to do the project. She was so busy sewing that she almost forgot to wash the twin dress—until she saw one of Buttons's chew toys on her bedroom floor and remembered the peeing incident.

She grabbed the dress from her hamper along with some of her other dirty clothes, threw it all in the wash, and then went back to sewing more outfits.

Marcus came to her room a few hours later. "Uh . . . you know that load of laundry you put in?"

Zoey had been so busy making doggie outfits,

she'd forgotten all about it. "Yeah, what about it?"

"Did you mean to put that dress in with it?"

Zoey got a sinking feeling in her stomach. "Dress? Why?"

"You'd better go take a look," Marcus said.

Zoey ran down to the laundry room. Marcus had taken out her clothes from the washing machine and put them on top of the dryer. Her twin dress was on top . . . but it looked like a different dress, a *ruined* one. The fabric was rippled and puckered and felt rough to the touch. It looked horrible.

"Oh no! What happened?" Zoey wailed. "Now what I am going to do?"

She put the rest of her clothes in the dryer and left the ruined dress on top. What a way to learn that the fabric she'd bought was probably dry-clean only! She would have to call Libby to tell her that Twinsies Day was off again—and maybe forever. Zoey wasn't eager to make that phone call, so she started sewing a dog outfit. Then she checked the Doggie Duds campaign page and found she'd gotten even more pledges. She would need to make a *lot* more rewards. Marcus agreed to take her to the office supply store to restock her supplies, and she spent the rest of the evening making rewards and addressing envelopes.

By the end of the night, her hands were cramped and she was exhausted.

"Come on, Zoey," Dad said. "Time for bed."

Mr. Webber was nudging her on the shoulder. She had fallen asleep at the dining table where she had been working. Running a business was hard work!

"I'm so tired," Zoey told Kate on the bus Monday morning. "I think I was stamping paw prints in my sleep."

"Doesn't the project end soon?" Kate asked.

"Yes, thank goodness. I'm not sure I can take much more success," Zoey said, pushing up her sleeves. "Look, I have paw prints all over my arms from the ink transferring."

Zoey slept on Kate's shoulder during the bus ride. When they arrived at school, Libby and Priti were waiting by the flagpole.

"Hi, guys!" Priti shouted. "Happy Monday!"

But Libby wasn't happy. She took one look at Zoey's outfit—a long-sleeved, striped sweater, polka-dot skirt, and white tights—and looked like she was about to cry.

"I thought today was Twinsies Day," Libby said when Zoey and Kate reached them.

"Oh no. I'm so sorry!" Zoey exclaimed. *How could I forget to call Libby?* she thought.

Priti's and Kate's eyes volleyed between Zoey's and Libby's faces.

Zoey took a deep breath and tried to explain. "It *was* supposed to be Twinsies Day. But I've been really busy with the Doggie Duds stuff. I didn't get a chance to wash the dress—to get Buttons's pee out of it—until last night. I didn't realize the fabric I used was dry-clean only, and the dress got completely ruined. I meant to call to tell you, but I got so crazy with making rewards for all the new Doggie Duds orders that I just . . . forgot."

Libby's expression didn't change. "What about today?" she asked. "You could have texted or something."

Zoey felt her heart sink to the floor. "I should

have, but I overslept, and all I could think about was finding something to cover up these paw prints on my arms, so Ivy wouldn't tease me about them. I'm really, really sorry, Libby. I should have called the second it happened."

Libby didn't say anything, which Zoey realized was even worse than if she had said something mean. She just stood there looking at her shoes—the shoes that went perfectly with her twin dress.

Priti broke the silence. "Hey, guys, cheer up! It's not the end of the world."

"And guess what?" Kate added. "I've been busy making things too." She reached into her backpack and pulled out a BFF bracelet that she'd made with all four bead colors: one for each of the four best friends. "This one is for you, Libby. We all felt awful that we didn't make one for you in the first place, so I remade all of ours with a fourth bead color: copper, to match your hair," she said, giving out the rest of the bracelets to Zoey and Priti and slipping the last one onto her own wrist. "How could we leave out one of our BFFs?"

"Really? I'm a BFF too?" Libby asked. She held

her wrist out next to Zoey's and Priti's arms. "I love it! You know, I did feel kind of left out when I saw you all had BFF bracelets and I didn't have one. And when I came back from getting frozen yogurt at the mall and you all stopped talking, it made me wonder if I was ever going to be a part of the group, you know?"

"You are!" Zoey said.

Then Kate spoke up. "And I wasn't a part of that conversation either, Libby."

"Priti and I just had to talk about something," Zoey added. "Something private."

"It's true," Priti said quietly. "Zoey had asked about my parents. You see, they're still having trouble, and I didn't want everyone to know."

"Oh!" Libby said. "I didn't know that. Well, BFFs don't have to share *everything*, I guess."

"So, are we good?" Priti asked. "I don't want any more drama."

"We're great," Libby said. "And, Zoey, maybe I can come over and help with your Myfundmaker project—and meet Buttons? It sounds like you have your hands full."

"We could all help," Kate said.

"Not that I'm inviting us all over to your house or anything, but how about a Doggie Duds working party this weekend?" Priti suggested.

"That would be awesome!" Zoey exclaimed, relieved. "You know what? You really are the best BFFs ever!"

CHAPTER 11

Doggies Are a *Girl's* Best Friend

You know how they say a dog is a man's best friend? Well, what about a *girl's* best friend? Buttons is definitely becoming my BFFF (my best *furry* friend forever). She is totally a*dog*able, just like Draper! When I finish making the last of the outfits for the local Doggie

Duds customers, I'm going to make us these matching outfits for whenever she comes to stay with us. I hope it's often.

But my human BFFs are pretty amazing too! Sew Zoey—and all the incredible adventures I've had because of starting this blog—would never have happened without them, and neither would Doggie Duds. So I'd like to thank my three best *human* friends forever—Kate, Priti, and Libby—for all their help with making the rewards. What would I do without you?

You were all so awesome about spreading the word, the orders went crazy in the last few days in the campaign, and we ended up being over 800 percent funded—way, way, way over our goal! Awesome, right? And thanks to the campaign, even after paying manufacturing costs and website processing fees, I've got money to buy fabric for new projects. Yay!!! Thanks especially to Fashionsista for telling me about Manufactory.com, because by the time the campaign came to an end, more than THREE HUNDRED OUTFITS were ordered.

If I had to make all the outfits and rewards myself,

I wouldn't be able to play with Buttons and take her for walkies (she's starting to learn that word now, so we have to start spelling it like we did with Draper), and that wouldn't be any fun now, would it?

Last but not least, an extra-special thanks to everyone who made super-duper pledges! You're sew cool, your names are listed—now and forever—on a new Sew Zoey Supporters page on the blog! Check it out!

"What have we got here, a full-scale production line?" Mr. Webber asked when he walked into the dining room on Saturday night.

"Pretty much," Zoey said. "Kate's in charge of cutting cards, Priti's stamping, Libby's addressing envelopes, and I'm sewing outfits."

"Can I offer some refreshments?" Mr. Webber asked. "Lulu brought over some delicious chocolate chip cookies this morning when she dropped off Buttons while she was antiquing."

"Yes, please!" Priti said.

"But we have to be careful not to get chocolate

on the rewards," Libby said. "Otherwise, it won't look very professional."

"I'll bring in napkins, too," Mr. Webber said, smiling. "I'm very impressed with how hard you all are working. You make a great team."

"We do make a great team, don't we?" Zoey said after her dad went back into the kitchen.

"The best team!" Priti said. "Ever!"

"Seriously, though, we do," Kate said. "Because we're all good at different things."

Kate is right, Zoey thought, looking down at her BFF bracelet. Each one of her friends brought something special to their group. When you put them all together, they were a really great combination.

After being fortified by Aunt Lulu's chocolate chip cookies, they managed to finish making all the rewards for Doggie Duds and addressing every single envelope. Everything was all stacked and ready to go into neat piles at the end of the dining room table, waiting for Zoey's dad to take them to the post office on Monday.

"Thanks so much for helping me," Zoey said. "It's such a relief to have those done!"

"That's what friends are for," Libby said.

"I just have three more local dog outfits to make tomorrow—one of which is Chester's," Zoey said. "The rest, the factory will make—yay!"

"So you can start making people clothes again?" Priti said hopefully.

Zoey laughed. "Yes. Glittery, sparkly people clothes, just the way you like them, Priti."

"Speaking of clothes, I was thinking, Zoey— since you love the dress from *Très Chic* so much, and the one you made got ruined, I'm going to give you mine," Libby said.

"For real?" Zoey exclaimed. "You would do that for me? I *love* that dress!"

"I would have done it before, but I was hurt because I thought you kept forgetting to be twins and it didn't mean as much to you as it did to me." Libby twisted her BFF bracelet on her wrist. "But I know that's not true."

Kate raised her glass of milk. "Here's to Zoey's business—and to BFFs!"

"To BFFs!" all the girls chorused, clinking their glasses together.

When Aunt Lulu had to go on another business trip a few weeks later, Zoey was thrilled to have Buttons back in residence at the Webber house— especially since she'd used some of the money from her newly replenished funds to get the cutest fabric to make the two of them matching outfits.

"Come on, Buttons," she said after putting on her dress. "It's time for these twinsies to go for walkies. Am I rightsie, Buttonsies?"

Buttons had learned "walkies" as well as Draper by now. She spun around three times and barked, her tail wagging furiously.

"Chill, Buttons! You have to put on your outfit first," Zoey said.

Buttons's tail didn't stop wagging, but she stood still, patiently waiting as Zoey put on her outfit. As soon as Zoey finished buttoning it, Buttons raced to the door and stood looking up at the handle.

Zoey clipped on her leash, and they went out into the neighborhood together, proud twins.

The first dog they encountered was the Labradoodle, Rusty, wearing the Draper.

"Doesn't he look handsome?" asked Mrs. Lynch. "And look at the two of you in your matching outfits. . . . Too adorable for words!"

"Thanks!" Zoey said.

A little farther along they bumped into Mrs. Silverberg and Princess, who was sporting the Buttons.

"Princess *loves* her outfit!" Mrs. Silberberg said. "And I love your matching outfits. Are you going to sell those, too?"

"I don't know," Zoey said. "The business was a lot of work. I learned a lot, but right now I'm going to concentrate on school and blogging."

"Well, if you ever decide to do another Myfundmaker campaign for those, count me in as a customer!"

"I will," Zoey said.

As Zoey and Buttons walked around the neighborhood, they saw more Draper outfits. Zoey still missed Draper terribly, but seeing all the neighborhood dogs wearing his outfit made it feel like he was still there in spirit. After all, the Draper outfit was everywhere she looked. Now, she and Buttons were walking their way to a whole new set of *very fashionable* adventures.

Don't leave Zoey—or her
wardrobe—hanging!
Keep reading for a sneak
peek at the next book in
the Sew Zoey series:

A TANGLED THREAD

Brand-New News!!!

The great thing about fashion is that there's always something NEW happening, right? Well, my life's like that too. I earned enough money from my Doggie Duds campaign to do some serious shopping for brand-new fabric, including the really pricey kind that I usually drool over from afar. I can't WAIT to get started on some new projects!

And speaking of new projects—drumroll, please—I'm also superthrilled to announce my next venture! Actually, it's a team thing. I'm going to be launching a collaboration Etsy store with another young designer, Allie Lovallo (with our parents monitoring, of course). Some of you might know her from our feature together on TresChic.com, or from her blog, Always Allie Accessories. The store will be called Accessories from A to Z, and—you guessed it!—we're going to be focusing on accessories! It's a pop-up shop that will be online for a limited time only, so get 'em while they're hot!

When we came up with the idea, I was going to sew clothes and she was going to make accessories, and we were going to call it Fashion from A to Z. The thing is, sizing clothes is complicated, while accessories are usually one-size-fits-most. So we decided to have an accessories store with some Allie stuff (Allie's the A) and some Zoey stuff (I'm the Z). It's going to be A for "awesome." As you can see from my sketch of some of the things I'm offering, I've already been hard at work. But I want to hear from you, readers. Let me know what else you'd like to see in our store!

We're launching the site as soon as we can, so this weekend I'll be doing all the last-minute work to get it ready. Tonight, though, I have a very important movie date—with two of my best friends! TGIF!

"More chocolate chips," Priti Holbrooke insisted. "Really, we need more."

Zoey Webber and Libby Flynn eyed each other skeptically, but then Zoey shrugged and went ahead and shook the entire bag of chocolate chips into the bowl. Priti grabbed a wooden spoon to fold them into the batter.

It was Friday night, and the three friends were at Libby's house, baking cookies and watching a movie, but they were barely paying attention to the screen. There was just too much to talk about! And too many chocolate chips to eat.

"We're going to have to rename these cookies chocolate chocolate-chip cookies," Libby said, laughing. "I've never used two whole bags of chips before!"

Priti smiled confidently as she folded melted chocolate into the batter. It went from a light tan color, to chocolate striped, to a deep chocolate brown. "My sisters and I always make them this way. Trust me."

Zoey spread out cookie sheets on the counter, and the three girls began dropping balls of dough onto them. As their hands moved back and forth, Zoey noticed that everyone was wearing their friendship bracelets. They had made the bracelets with a pattern using four different colors of metallic beads to represent each of the four best friends. There was rose gold for Priti, silver for Zoey, copper for Libby, and classic gold for their fourth BFF, Kate Mackey, who was at soccer practice that night, gearing up for state championships. Kate was Zoey's oldest friend in the world, and Zoey couldn't help feeling like there was something missing without her there.

"Kate would love these," Libby said.

"Yeah, she would," Zoey agreed. "When we were little we called her the Cookie Monster. Too bad she couldn't be here."

"Well, state championships are in a few weeks," Priti said. "And when it's over—and she scores the winning goal—she'll have more time to hang out! And eat cookies."

Zoey nodded. "True."

"You guys!" Priti shouted suddenly. Her hand flew to her mouth. "I can't believe I forgot to tell you!"

"Tell us what?" Libby asked. She slid the loaded cookie sheets into the oven, set the timer, and turned back toward Priti in one graceful move.

"I'm going to India!" Priti squealed. "Finally. For real."

"What? When?" Libby and Zoey both shouted at once.

Priti's eyes glowed. "My cousin is getting married in a few weeks, and we haven't seen most of our family in forever since they live all over the world. So all the relatives—from England, Canada, everywhere—are traveling to India for the wedding! It's going to be huge."

Immediately, Zoey began picturing a huge Indian wedding, with beautiful music and colors and food. "Oh, Priti, that sounds so cool!"

"I haven't been to a wedding since I was a flower girl in my uncle's wedding," Libby said. "You're going to have so much fun!"

"I know!" Priti said gleefully. "It'll be my first big traditional Indian wedding. My mom said the groom rides in on a white horse, and the bride and groom exchange garlands to show they accept each other as spouses. The celebration goes on for days. And everyone wears the most amaaaaazing saris. . . ."

Priti dug around in her bag to pull out her phone. She typed in a search term and held out the phone so Zoey and Libby could see as she scrolled through the pictures of saris. Despite the distracting smell of cookies baking in the oven, Zoey's mind immediately went into fashion overdrive.

"Oh my gosh, Priti!" she said, grabbing the phone so she could get a better look. "These are amazing! Look at the colors!"

Zoey kept shuffling through the pictures, completely entranced by the bright, jewel-tone colors; metallic embellishments; and sumptuousness of the fabrics. Her mind was already buzzing with ideas. How had she never noticed before that saris were the most beautiful dresses on Earth?

"They look complicated to put on," Libby said, studying one picture over Zoey's shoulder. "Are they one piece?"

"Some are, some aren't," Priti explained. "Some have a little top that's separate, and some just fold over one shoulder. It's, like, nine different steps to wrap one properly. My mom knows how, and my sisters, but I don't. There's a lot of tucking and pleating, and it takes a lot of patience!"

Zoey was barely listening. Already an idea was forming in her mind of how she'd design a sari, using one of those beautiful, beautiful fabrics, but making the style a bit more contemporary. . . .

sewZoey

Compared to middle school, fashion's a snap!

For sewing tips, excerpts, and more visit
SewZoey.com!